Visions from Venus

A Multidimensional Love Story

Book One ~ Where is Home?

By
Suzan Caroll

1stBooks – rev. 5/2/01

To Lamire

ACKNOWLEDGMENTS

I first began this book in 1992. Since then many people have assisted me in the many phases of its life. I first thank my husband for his continued support of my creative life. Without his encouragement I may not have had the courage to continue with such a long and soul-searching process. I thank my daughter, Julie Jordan, for listening to the stories as they came through and my son, Danny Jordan, for teaching me how to use the computer. I would like to thank Sal Rachele for his proof reading and encouragement for the first incarnation of this book. I also wish to thank Wyn Saunders for her support and vigilant editing as well as Kathleen Jason Moreau for her "slash and burn" editing. I thank Linda Mitchell for providing me with the grounding force of her wisdom and Virginia Palmer for being a wonderful sounding board and support system. Last, but not least, I would like to thank Shature for revealing her story to me.

PROLOGUE

THE STAIRWAY

I awaken—(Or have I just fallen asleep?)—to find myself on a stairway. Above me the stairs get brighter and more ethereal in form. Below me the stairs become darker and denser in form. I look at the stairs above me and feel a sparkle of love calling me to climb them. But when I try, I find that an inner pull urges me to turn and go down the stairs below me. I turn to look down the stairway and feel a fear that chills my heart. Why would I want to go down there?

"Because you already have," whispers a voice that seems to emanate from the sparkle of love.

"If I have been to that place," I ask, "why would I ever want to return?"

"You do not need to return," the voice breathes into my heart. "You have never left."

"No, that is not possible. I feel myself only here, upon this step."

"But you are on other steps as well. In fact, there is a you—many of you—upon every step. You see, each step represents a dimension, a plane of existence."

"If there are so many portions of myself, why don't I know about them?"

"Do you feel the pull from the steps beneath you?"

"Yes, I do."

"That pull is coming from the portions of yourself that are lost in the lower dimensions. They are lost because they believe they are alone. Because you have not freed them, you believe that you are alone."

"How can I free them when I appear to be lost myself?"

"Oh my one, you are not lost. You have found your higher voice—me. Your lost ones have sent you up this stairway, like a scout, to see if there was another way. Now you have found it. Go back and share your vision."

"Please don't make me leave. I remember it down there now and I want to stay here."

"You shall stay where you are, just as you will stay where you have been. You will not move, you will expand."

"Expand?"

"Yes, you see yourself now as a single point of awareness. Can you extend that awareness to imagine that you are standing on every step?"

I close my eyes and call upon my imagination. I have always had a vivid imagination. Oh yes, there they are. There is a person on every step. Each one has the same amount of light and density as the step they are standing on. They all look very different, but there is something about them that "feels" the same as well.

"Yes," the voice replies to my thoughts. "They all are of one consciousness. Can you feel how you and I are the same consciousness as well?"

It seems difficult for me to imagine that I could be the same as this wise and loving voice, but I close my eyes and try to make the connection. At first all I can perceive is the many voices of doubt, ridicule, and fear calling from the stairs below me. But gradually, I also feel love and support sparkling from the stairs above.

My perception expands. My consciousness expands. I feel stretched like a rubber band pulled so tight that it is ready to break. Tighter and tighter it pulls until I can barely stand the tension. Then, with a sudden SNAP, I understand.

I AM the loving voice that has guided me.

I AM the pull of fear and doubt.

I AM each person upon each step.

In fact, I AM each step and the imagination that created them.

I AM ALL IN ALL.

"Yes," resonates the loving voice from every person, every step, and every dimension. "We are a multidimensional being. It is our expansion from a singular consciousness to multidimensional consciousness that allows us to KNOW who we are."

DEFINITIONS

"**Dimensions**" are a means of organizing different planes of existence according to their vibratory rate. Each dimension has certain sets of laws and principles that are specific to the frequency of that dimension.

"**Consciousness**" represents awareness. The inhabitants of each dimension function clearly, easily, and with a minimum of resistance within that plane because their consciousness vibrates in resonance with the frequency of that dimension.

"**Multidimensional consciousness**" is the ability to be "conscious" of more than one dimension. To be multidimensional in our consciousness, we must remember that we have within us the potential to expand our perceptual awareness to the dimensions above and below our physical plane.

"**Unconscious**" means unaware of and unable to attend to internal and/or external stimuli within the inhabitants' own dimension or within another dimension. Third dimensional humans are largely unaware of their first dimensional, second dimensional, fourth dimensional and fifth dimensional selves. The human unconscious is best accessed through physical body messages, introspection, dreams, and meditation.

"**Conscious**" means aware of and able to attend to stimuli within the inhabitants' own dimension. The third dimensional self is conscious of what can be perceived by the five physical senses of sight, hearing, touch, taste, and smell.

"**Superconscious**" is a higher order of consciousness of the fifth dimension and above. From this state of consciousness, the inhabitants are able to be aware of and attend to stimuli within their own dimension as well as all the lower dimensions. The superconscious is innately multidimensional. The third dimensional self can become "conscious" of the superconscious self through meditation, prayer, and by surrendering to the guidance of higher dimensions.

For more about **Multidimensional Consciousness** please visit:

www.multidimensions.com

Table of Contents

Descent to the Third Dimension

Home in the Fourth Dimension

Return to the Third Dimension

Cast of Characters

Book One

Divine Complement-Male or female half of a Venusian androgynous being

    (Fifth dimensional Venus)

Lamerius -Androgynous Venusian being of Lamire and Lamira/Shature

    (Fifth dimensional Venus)

Lamire - The masculine Complement of the androgynous being, Lamerius

    (Fifth dimensional Venus and fourth dimensional Faerie)

Lamira - The feminine Complement of the androgynous being, Lamerius

    (Fifth dimensional Venus and fourth dimensional Faerie)

Shature - Lamira's Earthly name and the main character of the book

    (Third and fourth dimensional Earth)

Ramor - High Priest in Atlantis and Shature's mentor

    (Third dimensional Atlantis and fifth dimensional Venus)

Jatain - Shature's Atlantian mate

(Third dimensional Earth)

Vidann - Shature's Atlantian son

(Third dimensional Earth)

Vicor and Lateen - Shature's Atlantian friends

(Third dimensional Earth)

Tamara - Queen of Faerie

(Fourth dimensional Faerie)

Violet - Shature's Venusian flower

(Fifth dimensional Venus and fourth dimensional Faerie)

Malton - Shature's husband in post-Atlantian England

(Third dimensional Earth)

WHERE IS HOME?

There are still many of us
who cannot remember who we are.
We have worn our earthen bodies for so many eons
that we believe we are only physical
and that we are limited to these clay forms until we "die".

According to cosmic law,
as long as we believe in the third dimensional illusion
of limitation and separation,
that is our only experience.

Many of us have come from higher vibrations
to assist in the evolution of planet Earth
and to learn through the process
of third dimensional experiences.

The problem was
once we entered our physical forms
we began to forget.

Although we lost our memory

of who we truly are

and why we came to this planet,

we kept our full power,

at least for a while.

It was very dangerous to have

the limits of Earthly consciousness along with

with the limitless powers of the higher dimensions

because misuse of cosmic powers starts

a circular path that eventually returns to the sender.

Once we misused our powers

we began to lose them.

Then we really were "only physical".

As the collective consciousness of Earth

continued to drop further and further

from Spirit into Matter,

we plummeted deeper and deeper

into illusion and forgetfulness.

Before we knew it, we were enmeshed

In the evolutionary cycle

of planet Earth.

We would not be able to return Home,

to our true vibration,

until Earth consciousness had again risen

to a level where it would be possible

to receive messages from the divine kingdom

via the inner planes.

Some divine beings were able

to decrease their vibrations enough

so that a few Earthly beings,

who had raised their vibrations,

could perceive them.

However, Earth had so fallen

into fear and superstition that most communications

between divine beings and those on Earth

were greatly misunderstood or distorted.

And so the Light Beings waited!

Sometimes we hated the wait

and sometimes we loved it.

We learned that if we forgot about Home,

we weren't so lonely.

Therefore, most of us chose to forget.

And then, when we would least expect it,

as if in a dream,

we would remember something—

a feeling,

a brief picture,

a certain color or sound.

Then we would become very, very lonely.

We would want to go Home.

But we couldn't remember where Home was.

We only knew that is wasn't here.

We only knew that we didn't fit

and we didn't want to.

Book One

Where is Home?

In the beginning...

BOOK ONE

Descent to the Third Dimension

BOOK ONE

THE CHILD

A long time ago
in a land that no longer exists,
there was a temple high on a hill
which overlooked the valley and city below.

Far from the temple, in the Valley of Kenore,
there was a small foundling girl,
found by a simple and kind older
couple who had been unable to
have children of their own.

The small girl was different.
She was different from the couple,
different from her friends,
and different from her Self.
She spoke to beings that no one else
could see or hear.

The couple was very kind and would
not dream of reprimanding her.
But they worried.
She had been almost dead when they found her.
Perhaps her injury had affected her mind.

But, she was a great help.
When she was present,
the cows gave more milk,
the chickens laid more eggs
and the crops grew faster.

But still - she didn't "fit".
She was lonely,

so lonely that the simple couple
could feel it when they were near her.

Not that she complained.
No -- she appeared quite happy.
But yet, always, somehow lonely.

Perhaps she wanted to go HOME.

CHAPTER ONE

Separation

Where was she and why did she feel so confined, limited, alone? At the edges of her mind was something terrifying. She dared not let it in, at least not until she understood more about her circumstances. She looked around and discovered that everything was unfamiliar. The scenery had the same hard edges and heaviness she was experiencing in her own body. But wait! This was not her body. It was far too small and it seemed to be barely functioning. She felt a sharp pain in her head and a dull ache in her middle. Her heart center felt contracted and barely pulsed. The air that entered her mouth and nose was thick and tainted. What had happened? Where was she? Then, in a moment of clarity, she remembered!

She was Home, and her home was Venus. In her mind's eye, she saw the High Chancellor standing before her while the hundred and forty-four thousand stood around her. She could see the Chancellor's face clearly and hear the impassioned speech. The High Chancellor was commending them all for having the courage to volunteer to answer Earth's call for help.

"We are sending you to Earth in the hope that your light will help save the planet from total destruction, the same fate that awaits Atlantis. Earth's darkness far outweighs light now and times are very desperate. We don't know all the conditions there, but we know that it is very different from here. You will have a denser body that resonates to the vibration of the third dimension. Here, on Venus, we resonate to the fifth dimension. We live in unity consciousness with each other and with both polarities of ourselves. Therefore, we are all androgynous and our male and female components are housed within the same form. On third dimensional Earth the polarities are very extreme. There is good and bad, ugly and beautiful, and love and hate. Because of this separation of polarities, there is a possibility that your bodies will be either male or female.

"We are afraid that you may find life on Earth very difficult. We have learned that often there is a deep sense of limitation and a feeling of separation from others, and even from the other portions of yourself. Earth society has large segments of the population that are restricted in their ability to advance, and who spend their entire lives in service to those who are judged as being 'better'. We have no idea how it will feel to be only half of your total self or to be in a society which judges some of its members as having more worth than others. We only hope that you will be able to find your way to a temple or school where you can connect with other Venusians.

"We have arranged for all of you to take over another human's shell or to be born on Earth. We have tried to cover all age groups, as human forms do not live as long as we do here and their infants are totally dependent on adults for many years. Therefore, we need an entire range of ages in order to make a difference today as well as in the future.

"You all will have much work to do," continued the High Chancellor. "Your first, and perhaps most difficult task will be to remember who you are and why you are on Earth. Once you do so, it is important that you seek out the others and help them to remember as well. The younger your body is, the more difficult it will be to recall your mission, because the third dimensional brain will be less sophisticated than ours. We will have members stationed in all the temples and schools, and they will be on the lookout for the young Venusians as they grow up.

"We don't know how long it will be before the remainder of Atlantis sinks, but we know it will be soon. There have already been two major cataclysms that have taken huge portions of the continent into the sea. The loss of the rest of the continent is unavoidable, but we hope to assist in saving the planet. We have trained you well.

Now the time has come to begin your assignment. Atlantis recently suffered another large earthquake. There are many bodies, which we can heal enough for you to step into.

"I have one last, important message. As you know, you will be tying your karma into that of Earth. Therefore, you may have to finish your wheel of third dimensional incarnations on that planet. You are assigned there until the completion of their Grand Cycle, Earth year 2013 AD. We fear that you may not be able to make your final departure until that cycle is complete.

"We realize what a sacrifice this will be for all of you. If there is anyone now who does not wish to make the commitment, you may come to me quietly after the ceremony, and an alternate will take your place. We wish you all success in the completion of your mission."

With these final words, her vision faded. She felt very, very weary. She realized now why she felt so empty and alone. Where was her other half now? She guessed that it was masculine since she appeared to have a feminine form. Yes. It was all coming back to her now. She remembered when they were still one being before she entered the dying body. Lamerius was their name. The female polarity was known as Lamira and the male portion was Lamire. Lamerius, since they were complete then, saw the small female body below them. She appeared to be about ten years of age. Lamira entered the child's body first.

Oh, the pain! The sensations were so foreign and unexpected. Lamira instantly felt enclosed in a small, hard space. She had to fight her instincts to flee in order to complete her entry. She tried first to enter through the crown of the child's head, but it had been injured and was filled with blood. Lamira then tried to enter through the heart and was finally successful. However, she had to first experience a deep sense of fear. She had not felt fear on Venus, and she had to put her consciousness into the injured brain to find a title for what she was experiencing.

Yes, the child had been in terror. She had become lost and disoriented during the earthquake and had wandered to a cliff. Then there had been another tremor and she had fallen from the top of the cliff onto this rocky ledge. The child had hit her head as she fell. The last thing that crossed the child's mind before she lost consciousness was that she would die alone. Lamira used her own consciousness to heal the body she had entered and tried to assure the child that she was not alone. However, the child's Soul was gone -- leaving the memory of her terror embedded in the physical form. Lamira attempted to clear this fear before Lamire entered, but she felt a sense of urgency.

"Join me now," she cried.

"I can't," was his reply, "I have been trying. The body will only accept one of us. And, worse yet, something is pushing and pulling me away from you. I can't seem to stay in this environment very long without a body. They warned us of this possibility, but I couldn't imagine it would happen."

Lamire seemed as distraught as she was, but nothing worked. No matter how much they struggled, he couldn't enter the child's body with her. Instead, he was continuously pulled away.

"No, no," she implored. "You can't leave me here. I am only half of myself and alone on this foreign planet. You must stay!! Don't leave me."

Lamira was getting hysterical. She was trying to follow Lamire, but did not yet know how to function in her new form. The terror! The terror of being only half of her total Self!

"Come back, come back," she cried to Lamire.

As she lost consciousness, she saw him being pulled away from her to some distant destination.

When at last she awoke, she found herself in some form of a bed with two elderly looking people tending her body. The woman sat on the bed and appeared to be trying to feed her while the man stood behind her. They uttered some words that were unrecognizable to her, and the expressions on their faces changed as they spoke. Again, it took her a moment to remember what had happened, and as she did, it hit her like a sharp pain. But, with the pain of the recollection came an awareness of her greater self.

She was not the small child whose body she now inhabited. She was a fifth dimensional Venusian on a mission with her comrades to help the Earth in its time of need. Her third dimensional form still felt foreign and restrictive, and she could barely move the small, weak body. She clung to the experience of her own consciousness just outside of and within the child's physical form. She focused her mind to access the higher powers she had possessed on Venus, but there was too much disturbance in the atmosphere for her to sense anything outside of the small room. She could only read the minds of the couple before her.

She wondered if this was the child's family. No, she sensed that the man had found her when he was searching the mountainside for the injured and lost. She could sense that the man and woman were kind, but they didn't seem to register much thought. They were very simple and lived day to day off the land without questioning or philosophical ideation. Lonelier than ever, she swallowed a bit of the warm liquid offered to her by the woman and gave her body up to sleep.

Gradually, over several months, she gained strength. She learned how to move her body within the dense atmosphere of Earth and how to form the messages she sensed in her mind into the language of the couple. She waited and waited for her other half to return or somehow contact her, but he was nowhere around. The grief of losing him was even greater than the grief of leaving behind her beloved Venus. Perhaps, she thought, he just could not find her. So, as soon as she was well enough, she returned to the cliffs whenever the couple wasn't looking. She would curl her knees up in her arms and look off sadly into the sky, but Lamire never came to her.

The couple became very worried. This child did not seem normal. Physically, her body had healed, but something seemed wrong with her mind. She barely spoke to them, but often spoke to the farm animals. They had even seen her talking to plants and into the sky. When they asked her what she was doing, her face would cloud over like a brewing storm and she would shake her head and walk off. It was not that the child was not helpful. In fact, the plants and animals that she tended seemed to grow healthy and strong. But, she barely spoke to people and in her sleep she would call the name Lamire, again and again. When they questioned her, she only replied, "He is gone."

As much as the couple had wanted a child, they realized they could not help her anymore and decided to take her to the Temple. Perhaps there she could be healed. But more tremors and rough weather made it impossible to leave for several months. During that time, the child did not improve. In fact, she seemed worse. However, she did seem physically well enough for the two day walk to the temple. So, one morning before dawn, they set off.

When they arrived at the Temple, the couple noticed that the child seemed to cheer up at its sight. There were still so many injured people making their way to the Temple that they had to wait for another two days before they could be seen.

Finally, it was their turn. A lovely temple Priestess called them into a small room to interview them and determine how they could best be helped. The room was circular with benches along the walls. The man and woman sat on one side of the room and the Priestess sat across from them. The child lingered just inside the doorway, looking at the floor.

"She is always like that," spoke the man. "I found her on a cliff by our farm after the last earthquake. She was almost dead, but my wife nursed her back to health. She barely talks and is always running back to that cliff like she is looking for something. We have done all we can. We thought maybe you could help her."

His wife nodded in agreement.

"We were very happy to have a child in our home, as we could not have children of our own. However, she does not seem happy and is becoming more and more distant."

15

The Priestess walked over to the girl and knelt before her.

"Can you tell us what you are looking for on the cliff?" the Priestess asked in a soft and gentle voice.

The girl looked into the eyes of the Priestess and instantly felt at home. She could feel that the Soul of this woman was more akin to hers and she felt she could trust her.

"I am looking for my other half. He could not enter this body with me."

A look of recognition covered the Priestess' face while the elderly couple shook their heads in dismay.

"You see," said the man. "Perhaps it was from her injuries, but she doesn't seem to be right in the head."

"You did the correct thing to bring her here," spoke the Priestess. "I think that we can help her. Can you leave her here?"

"That is why we came," spoke the woman. "There is nothing else that we can do for her."

"What you have done so far has been very kind indeed."

The girl wanted to stay in the Temple but realized that she had never thanked the couple for saving her life. She had done nothing but worry about herself. She then walked over to the couple, who were still seated, and gave each of them a warm hug.

"Thank you for helping me. I have been so sick and confused that I have only thought of myself. Without you two, I would have died."

The couple seemed surprised by the maturity of the girl's words when she had hardly spoken in all the months she had lived with them, but they were very grateful for the girl's acknowledgment of their kindness. They each gave her an embrace in return.

"Perhaps we will return one day to visit you," spoke the woman.

"Yes," smiled the girl.

She knew she would never see them again.

As soon as the couple left the room, the Priestess instructed the child to follow her up many stairs and through many hallways. Since she had come to the Temple, there had been an expansion of her fifth dimensional awareness. The architecture of the Temple vaguely resembled the Violet Temple on Venus, but mostly it was the vibration that was familiar. She could tell before she even entered the main door that there was a resonance in the Temple that was not present in the valley where the couple lived. As she followed the Priestess, she pondered her new life. In all the time she had spent with the couple, she had been so involved in learning how to live on third dimensional Earth without Lamire, that she had lost contact with her higher awareness.

Being inside of a third dimensional body was very difficult for her. She had almost wished that she had forgotten who she really was so that she could better adapt to the small, dense form that she was now confined to. However, she could not forget her other half. If she could hold his memory, she still might be able to make contact with him. Sometimes even Lamire blurred from her mind. She was so intent on learning how to walk without the flowing, floating sensation of Venus that she had to limit her senses of perception. If she did not, she became overloaded with the thoughts and feelings of all those around her. She seldom spoke to the couple because their minds invaded hers and pulled her thinking down into the routine acts of survival.

Even though she saw few people besides the couple, the atmosphere was dense with fear and suffering. To make matters worse, the fear that had remained in the child's body, coupled with her own loneliness, left her feeling alone, hopeless and afraid. She had tried to use her mind to function with her fifth dimensional powers, but they were lost in random thoughts and negative emotions of her third dimensional body.

The girl was so absorbed in her own thoughts that she almost bumped into the Priestess when she stopped abruptly in front of a large door in one of the Temple's towers.

"You will soon meet our High Priest, Ramor," said the Priestess as she tapped upon the heavy door.

"Yes?" came a strong voice from beyond the door.

"I think I have one of the children. Can you see her now?"

Lamira was suddenly aware of the child's body that she inhabited and held her breath for fear that Ramor would not want to see her. It seemed to be a very long time before he responded.

"You may show her in."

His voice sounded clear and kind, and Lamira relaxed. The Priestess unlatched the door and allowed it to swing open.

"He will see you now," she said as she stepped back and beckoned for the child to enter. Just before Lamira crossed the threshold, the Priestess touched her on the shoulder. Lamira turned her head and looked up at her face.

"Welcome," said the Priestess with a friendly smile.

Lamira smiled in response and entered the room. At first, all she could see was a bright golden light. Slowly she realized that the light was the aura of a man sitting across the room in a large chair. He had white hair, a white beard and his piercing blue eyes glistened as he looked into her face. "He must be one of us," she thought.

Ramor rose when she entered the room and invited her to sit down in a chair across from him. Though the room was small, the walk across seemed very long to Lamira. Knowing that Ramor was a Venusian flooded her heart with joy. However, it also brought back all the loneliness and pain that she had tried to repress while in the valley with the couple.

"Yes, I am one of you," he replied as they both sat down. Apparently, he had read her thoughts and had seen her essence despite the small human form that now encased it.

"You must be the greeter the High Chancellor spoke of."

"Yes," he replied. " I am one of them."

"I was afraid that you would not recognize me as one of the Venusians," said Lamira.

Ramor seemed to study her for a while.

"I can see from your aura that you have had a very difficult time. I am sorry. You are safe now, and we can set you on your path of service. Since your body is that of a child's, you will have to live a child's life here until it matures. Do not fret though as there are others in your situation, and they will be great company for you. I am glad you are here, but I apologize because I must leave now to teach a class. May I show you to your quarters? We will have much time to talk later."

But as he stood she stopped him, "Wait! I must first find out about my other half. He could not enter this Earth form with me, and I have heard nothing of him since he was pulled away from me."

Ramor sat down again and looked directly into her Soul. His eyes sent her such understanding and compassion that Lamira's breath caught, and her eyes filled with tears. Ramor reached across the short distance between them and gently touched her on the knee.

"Our Venusian family was afraid that this would happen. Apparently, it depends upon the personal evolution of your host body. Even though I outwardly appear to be a man, my entire essence lives within this form. The body that I entered was that of a High Priest who was healthy and willing to vacate his physical form for me. He had meditated many years to gain contact with his Complement. Therefore, his body was able to hold both polarities of my being. However, you entered a peasant child with no spiritual training, and one who was on the verge of death. I'm sorry this has happened to you. I can see that it was a terrible experience. However, we can teach you how to communicate with your Complement."

Ramor pulled a small cloth from the folds of his robe and gently handed it to her. Lamira dried her eyes and tried to hand it back.

"Please keep it," he said. "There are many tears here on Earth. Allow this to be my first gift to you."

21

Lamira smiled and accepted her gift.

"What did the couple call you?" he asked still looking into her eyes.

"They just called me child,'" she responded.

"How were you known on Venus?"

"We were known as Lamerius. Lamire was the name of our male energy and Lamira was the name of our female energy."

"Should we call you Lamira then?"

"Oh, no. That name would only remind me that part of me is missing. I think I need a new name for my new life as a third dimensional female."

"Follow me," he said warmly as he stood. He reached his strong hand out to welcome hers. "We will get you a new name for your new life."

CHAPTER TWO

Reunion

Her name was to be Shature. Ramor told her it meant "ability to stand alone". She thought it was a pretty name and guessed he picked it for her to help her cope with the absence of her Complement. "Complement" was what the other Venusians in human form called the other polarity of their one self that lived in the higher dimensions. Shature had been told that long ago Earthlings had been able to communicate with their Complements and some even lived as androgynous beings. However, times had grown very dangerous and evil on Atlantis. There was so little loving, spiritual guidance and so much temptation for selfishness and ill-doing that the vibratory rate of the planet had dropped. Hence, the resonance had become so low that most people were either only male or only female.

It was hoped that the other polarity of self that lived in the higher dimensions could serve as a kind of inner guide or conscience. Although most of the people were totally unaware of the higher aspects of themselves, a component of their Souls could still remain pure in the higher dimensions. This other half, or Divine Complement, could then assist them to be receptive at times, such as during sleep, crisis or upon death. Those who were able to study in the Temple's mystery schools could learn how to regain communication with their Divine Complement and, in so doing, create constant inner guidance, companionship, and comfort.

Shature was very anxious to learn this communication, but she had other things to learn first. She studied diligently in her classes, and the years passed by quickly. One of the first things that she had to learn was to raise her consciousness above that of the masses and, in fact, above that of many of the priests and priestesses. There were many people who used the cloak of spiritualism as a boon to their personal power. These initiates were not healers or artists. However, they had gone through their mystery schools and had gained great powers to manipulate the forces of nature and the unconscious forces within the minds of others.

There were three schools of learning in Atlantis. The Light Robes, the Gray Robes and the Dark Robes. The Light Robes studied unity consciousness and unselfish service to the Oneness of All Life. The Dark Robes studied the attainment of wisdom for their own selfish purposes and used malefic Magic for selfish acquisition, no matter what the cost to others. The Gray Robes sought to find a balance between the Light and the Dark Robes. Unfortunately, lately they had focused their learning more in the direction of the Dark Robes and had joined the forces of evil that were overtaking the planet.

Shature had great difficulty with the dark forces within her own physical body. On Venus, their vehicle was fifth dimensional and of pure light. The resonant vibration of Earth was much lower than on Venus. In order for her to hold her life force in her physical form, she had to adopt a consciousness far below that which she held on Venus. Also, her Earth body was that of a child and the concept of childhood was quite foreign to her. On Venus, the newer bodies were somewhat smaller and less developed than the older bodies, but they were soon independent. Since the Venusian environment was much safer, the young were free to make most of their own decisions and choices soon after their incarnation began.

On Earth, those who did not know her true identity treated her like one who had no awareness of what was best for her. When she was among others of the hundred and forty-four thousand who came down to Atlantis, she could relax a bit, but as a group they all had to be careful. If the wrong people found out who they were, it could mean their lives. The forces of darkness wanted Atlantis to stay the way it was. They thought only of the present and refused to look at the long-term effect of their actions. If they found out that the Light Robes had received reinforcements from Venus, there would be mayhem. It would then be difficult for the Venusians to carry out their tasks of rescuing those who were ready to hear the truth. Already, a few of the Venusians had "disappeared". Their friends could use their telepathy to follow them to a certain point, but then, they seemed to disappear. When Ramor was asked what had happened, he only said,

"They were found out. From this dimension it is difficult to tell if their essences were able to return Home or not. There is even a rumor that certain Souls have been trapped in special crystals that the forces of darkness control."

"Does that mean that the evil ones know who we are?" they asked.

"I'm not sure. I'm hoping that they only saw that these Souls had enough potential to be dangerous to their present power structure and they did not know about their Venusian identity. I must stress-- be careful. Do not let all of yourself show, as it is too dangerous. Look closely into the aura of others before you interact with them. We must all protect ourselves, and each other, so that we can achieve our primary goal--to save this planet from complete destruction!"

"How will we do that?" they questioned.

"I don't know," was his reply. "I only hope that at the appropriate time it will become evident."

Shature's studies at the Temple proceeded slowly. Before she could learn to communicate with her Complement, Shature had to learn all about these evil priests and priestesses and how to protect herself from them. She learned that their powers were drawn from the lowest Astral Plane. Between the third dimension of physical Earth and fifth dimensional Venus was the fourth dimension, also known as the Astral Plane. The Astral Plane amplified and radiated the emotions and thoughts of both the third and the fifth dimensions. There were many levels of vibration within the fourth dimension. The Lower Astral Plane held the emanations of Earthly emotions and intentions, and the Higher Astral Plane held the emanations of the fifth dimension.

In order to raise her consciousness to the fifth dimension, where she could fully access her Venusian powers, she had to learn how to forge a path through the Lower Astral Plane. The Lower Astral Plane, being the lowest resonance of the fourth dimension, was filled with the fear and anger of the newly dead who were unable to connect with their Spirit Guides or higher dimensions of themselves before or during death. There were also discarnates in that plane that did not want to accept the termination of their physical life, and they sought any avenue to return to a life that was now over for them. Before Shature could reach the higher planes of consciousness where her other half may be awaiting her, she had to learn how to protect herself from the dark psychic forces of this plane. Fear was the greatest problem. There was so much fear emanating from Earth that the Lower Astral Plane became impassable and working her way through this lowest plane of consciousness was much more difficult than she could have imagined.

Even though few Earthlings confessed an awareness of the fear that was a part of their everyday existence, their auras revealed that they knew something was amiss. There were murders and burglaries, something unheard of on Venus. Since their fear was not expressed, it was instead acted out as anger that held the desperation of their fear of survival. Groups of people gathered together, presumably for safety, and then attacked other groups. Fear and evil permeated the air, twisting the focus of even these safety groups, and the solution became a part of the problem. The fear, desperation, and anger were contagious and threatened to lower Shature's consciousness as well as the consciousness of the other Venusians.

No wonder Lamire had to leave her. Shature's earth body actually served as protection against the negative psychic energies that engulfed the planet. When Lamire could not enter it with her, his essence was vulnerable, without protection. The Dark Robes, and now the Gray Robes as well, could trap and use life force if it wasn't held within a vehicle. They could even steal the life force from the living if that person were weak enough. Therefore, she had to keep herself strong. This was difficult because she constantly felt lonely and sad. These emotions eroded away at her strength and clouded her mind. She missed her other half and she missed Venus.

Ramor realized Shature's problem and kept her busy. Since her body was now thirteen Earth years, she looked mature enough to leave the Temple. Therefore, one of her tasks at the temple was to go to the marketplace with some of the house staff. She was chosen for this job because she had retained her empathic and telepathic abilities and could assess the feelings and thoughts of the population. She had to be careful. It was difficult to psychically read others without allowing their negativity to enter her. Sometimes she could do this, but if she was at all tired, ill, or harbored any strong emotions, she could not shield herself from others' negativity. When this happened, it would take her many days to clear out her aura and regain her center. At the times she was "tainted," she was very susceptible to human diseases-- physical or emotional. She would then have to go into isolation until the danger was over.

Another reason for her to go to the marketplace was to identify other Venusians. Not all were as fortunate as she was to be taken to the Temple, and some could not even remember who they were. However, their auras would tell her that they were Venusians, even though they could not. Shature always kept her consciousness open in search of a clue as to Lamire's whereabouts. If he had taken another body, and she found him, she could join with him as a mate. Her constant searching and sadness were beginning to show in her attitude and in her health to the point that even her good works were becoming overshadowed.

One day, she received a summons from Ramor. Once again, as she entered into his presence, she was aware of his beautiful golden aura. "That's because he is with his Complement," she thought jealously, forgetting how well he could read thoughts.

"That is why I have summoned you here," he said sternly.

Shature realized that he had read her thoughts again, and she was ashamed and embarrassed. She made no reply and hung her head.

"I realize your pain," he continued in a softer voice, "but your obsession with finding your Complement is endangering you and those around you. You underestimate the power of the evil priests. Many of the Black and Gray Robes can also read minds, and they will begin to wonder why you would have such thoughts. Already, as you know, several of us have disappeared. They are certainly suspicious of something."

"You have to realize that the person you are now *is* all of you. You must stop desiring that which you cannot have at this time. It only distracts you from your growth. In allowing yourself to fall into sadness and depression, you are moving your consciousness in the opposite direction from that which you wish to realize. If you continue to fall into your emotions, you will never be able to move your consciousness through the Lower Astral Plane to communicate with your Complement. Also, the forces of darkness will surely see your leaking psychic field as one which they can steal or use. You are so involved in your personal pain that you have lost sight of the severity of this situation."

She was shocked by his words. She had no idea she had been so transparent. Yet she still had to ask him some questions, even though she knew it would make him angry.

"Does this mean that I will never be able to join with Lamire in this life?"

"Yes," he replied firmly. "In fact, you may never be able to join him until the grand cycle is over and you are ready to return Home."

The enormity of this statement took her breath away.

"However," he continued, "You will probably only be aware of your separation for this lifetime. By your next life you will be an Earthling and the separation will feel as natural to you as it does to everyone else. You will be able to meet with your Divine Complement in your dream-state, or deep meditation, and in-between incarnations."

"Will my other half always remain in the higher planes while I struggle down here?"

"No, my dear, just as it acts as a beacon for you while you are embodied, you will act as a beacon for it when it is embodied and you are in the higher planes. I know that your next question is whether the two of you will ever be together on the physical plane. The answer is--perhaps. However, that can be a very dangerous arrangement because if both of you fall into darkness, your Soul (which encompasses both of you) will suffer greatly and the recovery will take many, many lifetimes."

"Why didn't they explain this to us on Venus?"

"As I said before, we did not exactly know it. Now that so many of you have arrived and more time has passed, we are more aware of the situation. Actually, you are among the more fortunate. Many others are not even aware they are Venusians. We have decided to allow them to make their own discoveries because the realization of the separation from their Divine Complement is so agonizing."

Shature was glad she remembered her Complement, even though it was painful. At least she had a memory of her full potential and something concrete to work towards. Somehow realizing that she was not alone in her pain, and actually better off than others, helped her to stop feeling sorry for herself. She realized that she had been selfish and was actually endangering others with her negative attitude. It was time to face reality, get over her grief, and focus on fulfilling her mission. Ramor had helped her to get out of her problems and regain her sense of purpose. She apologized honestly for her behavior and left his presence with a new attitude and sense of direction.

After her talk with Ramor, Shature was able to expand her service for the forces of light. She had an ability to tune into the vibrations of the Earth and could determine when and where the next tremor or major earthquake would occur. Then healers and other helping units could go to that site to be of assistance. Although they had to be careful whom they warned to avoid arousing too much suspicion, they could use their information to calculate how much longer the continent would survive. This gave the rescue team time to relocate those who wished to leave for safer areas. They could also buy time for the continent by moving to the areas of darkness and performing healings on the Earth.

The light workers had discovered that wherever there had been an earthquake, there had previously been actions of Black Magic by the Black and Gray Robes or excessive use of the power crystals by the rulers and wealthy. Each disaster radiated through valleys, waterways, or marshes from the Central Crystal, which was the main power source for the entire continent. The members of the Temple had warned the political figureheads repeatedly that the overuse of the power sources was causing underground weaknesses. None of them cared, however, because they had lifestyles to maintain and possessions that needed power.

One of the main drains on the Central Crystal was the Life Regenerator. This was a unit which revitalized the life force of individuals who entered it. It lengthened their life as well as healed them of diseases. This unit consumed vast quantities of power and was constantly in use. Once everyone was allowed to use the Life Regenerator if they petitioned and proved that they had not yet finished the service of that lifetime. Now it was a service that was bought. Therefore, only the wealthy could afford its use, and even they had to wait from six months to a year. However, enough money could buy a position at the head of the waiting list. These wealthy and lazy people did not want to care for themselves properly or face the Karmic Board at their death. They were making their own lives a little more comfortable and ruining the lives of all the generations to follow them!

Once the Central Crystal belonged to everyone. It had been brought to Atlantis long ago from the ancient land of Mu. It was said that they had received the Crystal from the first star people that populated Earth. Now, the wealthiest members of the ruling class had bought the Crystal. The money that they received from the use of the Life Regenerator lined their pockets and assured their positions as the real power behind the throne.

As Shature's studies and service at the Temple progressed, she began to feel a growing peace of mind. She learned that she could acknowledge the conditions on the planet without allowing them to affect her emotionally. As she gained this ability she was able to learn more truths. The realization of truth, she determined, was dependent on one's ability to embrace it without agitation. After she had accepted the loss of Lamire, everything else was easy in comparison. When she released her constant search for him, she began to allow herself to make friends. These friends brought her joy. They would sit together at meals and in their free time laughing and enjoying each other's company.

Vicor was one of her first friends. Vicor was also a Venusian and had taken the body of a boy at the same time that Shature had entered her young female body. They met at the temple several years later when they both studied with Ramor. Vicor was very virile, full of life and laughter, and seemed to always see the positive in every situation. Although he was a bit arrogant, his heart was pure and his Soul shined through his deep brown eyes. Vicor pursued a friendship with Shature and included her in his large group of friends. His open, friendly manner melted the ice around her heart and helped ease the anger that she had been working so hard to release.

Lateen was the first female friend she made. She was quite short with a petite body. She appeared very delicate with her wispy blond hair and light blue eyes, but she emanated a deep courage that Shature admired. Shature probably liked Lateen so much because she was much like her. Lateen was shy, quiet, and often took long walks alone in nature. In fact, it was on one of Shature's solitary walks that she first met Lateen. At first, they avoided each other, but they both enjoyed the same places and kept running into each other no matter where they went. Finally, they laughed and began to talk. It was with Lateen that Shature could share her deepest fears and insecurities. Lateen was also aware that she had lost her Complement and shared Shature's sense of loss and loneliness. They discussed their different experiences and feelings and found great comfort in each other. Shature learned that there were some things that a woman can only share with another woman. It was difficult to only be half of herself, but she was learning more about her feminine self than she had ever known on Venus.

And then there was her very special friend, Jatain. He was the closest to her of all her friends. There was a feeling between them that felt familiar, like they had known each other before. He did not remember his entry into his body nor the initial loss of his other half, but he gradually grew to remember his consciousness on Venus and how it was different from Earth's. Shature and Jatain were able to help each other greatly. Shature helped him to remember his first entry into a human form, and he assisted her in overcoming her pain and loneliness. As the years passed, their friendship grew. They became constant companions. They ate together, went to Temple classes together, and spent their free time together. Often they walked in the hills around the Temple and swam in the pools that were still clear and fresh on the Temple grounds. They talked about everything, laughed, studied and meditated together. With every day, Shature's pain diminished and she allowed herself to open her heart to her dear friend and companion.

Before they knew it, Shature and Jatain were at the age of initiation, which was twenty-one in Earth years. They both were excited and anxious. Prior to their initiations, they fasted on water and juice for seven days. They each stayed in isolation on the Temple grounds reserved for that purpose to await their vision. There was an area for women in a lovely garden and a different area for men in a nearby courtyard. This segregation of men and women reminded Shature of her loss of Lamire and brought up her old feelings again. She tried to control her anger, but the sorrow of her separation from Lamire distracted her from her meditations. The more she fasted and meditated, the more hurt and angry she became.

She needed to consult with someone because she was obviously doing something wrong. This was to be a time of purification, not a time of bringing up old painful memories.

By the end of the sixth day, she was so uncomfortable with her emotions that she felt as though she might explode. Shature thought she had released these feelings, but they now seemed stronger than ever. She began to pace back and forth across the grounds of her isolated garden. As she did so, she worked herself into an ever-deepening trance. The anger grew, as did the sadness, to a state that was almost unbearable. As the emotions grew stronger her trance deepened until her outer world was blocked out by her inner vision.

She saw herself walking down into a deep, dark tunnel. As she descended into the tunnel her anger and sadness began to turn to fear. Fear of what—she did not know. It was raw fear without reason or purpose. She saw it before her like an energy field that filled the tunnel around her. She realized that she had created a place within herself that was an echo of the environment outside her beloved Temple.

"No!" she cried. "I cannot do this to myself. I am to be a Priestess. I must release my pain."

Then, as if in response to her words, a huge golden light ignited before her. Shature stood frozen to that spot in awe of the phenomenon before her. As she stood transfixed, the blazing light gradually took on a vaguely human form.

"If you are ready to release your suffering, you can surrender it to me," spoke a voice that radiated from the light.

"But how?" was her response.

"If you can believe that you are not alone and can accept that you have chosen all of your experiences, then you can release your suffering. Your emotions are the carriers of your third dimensional experiences. They bring you the lessons that you must learn in order to fulfill your destiny. Once you have learned your lessons and taken responsibility for the choices you have made, you can surrender the painful emotions to the light."

"But what are my lessons. I do not know them."

The light began to fade.

"No," called Shature. "Do not leave me alone again."

"I am not leaving you," responded the voice within the light. "You are choosing to push me away."

"I don't want to push you away. How am I doing it.?"

"Feel yourself. Does your energy pull me to you or push me away."

At first Shature did not know what the voice meant, but she could see that her confusion was making the light grow dimmer.

She knew that she must still her mind and listen to the light's message. She tuned into the core of her being and allowed a tone to arise with her breath. The tone was dissonant and she coughed when she tried to release it. She held out her hand and looked at her aura. It was dim and close to her body. Yes, she understood now that she could not accept the light in her current state. All that she could see was the light before her and the tunnel of darkness behind her. Did she choose to fall back into the tunnel from whence she came or was she ready to move forward into the light? With that thought, the light grew brighter. Shature knew that it was responding to her ability to accept responsibility for her life. She attempted to move her physical body toward the light, but found that she could not command it. She did not know if she was standing or sitting, nor how long she had been in the tunnel.

"No," she thought. "This tunnel is an illusion. But the light is real because it is the force of life that I have not allowed into my physical form. I have chosen to allow all of the emotions that I have felt since I came to this dimension, but I have not allowed the force of this light to balance them."

"You came to Earth to clear the darkness and replace it with light," explained the voice in the now radiant light. "However, first you had to understand the nature of darkness. When you were on Venus, you lived in a state of unity and joy. Until you came to third dimensional Earth you had not experienced separation from the Oneness. When you experienced this separation you felt fear, sadness and anger for the first time.

"In order for you to complete your mission on Earth, you must learn to understand and become master of these emotions. Then you can release the illusion of separation by remembering your true nature. If you can master your pain enough to release your darkness into my light, you can assist in releasing the darkness of the planet as well."

"Your words are wise and I will heed them. May I ask who you are?" asked Shature.

"I am you."

"Do you mean you are my Complement?"

"No, I am you -- complete!"

"But that can't be," she argued. "You are so powerful and serene, and I am insecure and afraid."

"There is a portion of us that is insecure and afraid. Your consciousness in now limited to that portion. You can expand your consciousness to encompass the portion that I AM!"

"How do I do that? I have tried and tried."

41

"You do not need to try to achieve that which has always been yours. All you need to do is to remember."

Yes. Shature realized now that during her eleven years on Earth, she had been so busy learning and trying that she had forgotten much of her life on fifth dimensional Venus. Could it be so simple that all she had to do was remember? But where would she begin? There was so much. There was the floating gardens that surrounded the Violet Temple and the beautiful pink shores that caught the Waters of Light. There was also the special cove where, in her androgynous form of Lamerius, they had meditated and relaxed.

Yes, Lamerius! She had forgotten the name that she and her Complement used when they joined into one being on Venus, because she was afraid that remembering it would bring her torment. But it was the forgetting that brought the pain, pain of separation and loss. She remembered how proud they had been to take on the challenge of assisting Earth and the camaraderie of the hundred and forty-four thousand. They were as one mind and one heart. She had missed that. But she had found it again with Ramor, Vicor, and Lateen...and with Jatain. She was surprised to find that she could remember times from her third dimensional life that brought her power and serenity.

The third dimension had not been completely bad. The relationships with her friends in the Temple were strong and warm.

42

They were mostly Venusians, but they also wore the clay bodies of the third dimension. The fear of Earth had made it difficult for her to trust. However, when it was safe to trust, the fear made the trust seem even more powerful. She thought of Lamire and how it felt to be one with him, and she thought of how it felt to be close to Jatain. It was different with Jatain, but it was good. It was serene and safe. They were two separate bodies, but their love united them.

"I do remember," she called to the voice in the light. "I remember that I am not separate from you. I am not limited to the pain and fear that surrounds me. I am you and you are I. We are One!"

In response to her call, the light, which had been in a vague human shape, moved closer and closer until it was directly in front of her.

"Step into me," it said, "and I will step into you. You are physical, and I am spirit. Together we are ONE."

With this final message, the vision faded, leaving only stillness and peace. Her pain and anger were absorbed into the light and the light had been absorbed into her. The light held her darkness and the darkness was a portion of her light.

Shature's initiation vision served as a shield for her. Whenever she began to fall into her negativity she remembered herself --

complete. As a complete Soul, she was above pain and self-pity. She could rise above the consciousness that was vulnerable, and thereby stay above personal and planetary destruction. She began to see her environment not so much as a place of which she was a part, but as a place she moved through and worked in while in her waking state. Her dreams became more vivid. Before her initiation, her dreams had been disturbing and vague. Now they were very clear and often gave her messages that she took into her waking life. She had one recurring dream in which she saw herself standing before a stone wall. She heard a great rumbling but was unafraid. She knew the waters would come, but she would not die. She knew that this message was for her alone and that she couldn't tell anyone, even Jatain.

Jatain had also completed his initiation. She saw less of him now, but when she did, it was different, more serious. They had both gone into their own darkness and come out stronger and wiser. She believed that soon she would mate with him. They brought great comfort to each other, and their friendship grew stronger every day. She wondered if her Complement would be jealous, or if he was above those lower emotions. Some day she would communicate with him and ask. For now, she had to live the life she had and stay out of old her disappointment.

One day while she was in the marketplace (she was now the main buyer for the Temple), she came upon an interesting discovery. There was a group of people who all had the same kind of aura — one which was very clear and loving. These people moved throughout the marketplace, supposedly buying, in groups of two or three. On a physical level, they had nothing in common. On a higher level, however, she could see that they were in constant communication with each other. She knew she had to be very careful, as what looked like a friend could, in fact, be an enemy. She had to find a way to communicate with them. She moved to the group closest to her, ostensibly to buy something at a nearby booth, and accidentally bumped into one of them. Apologizing, she took that moment to look into its eyes to feel its essence. This being was not an Earthling, and it was complete, both male and female. She felt a great rush of love and compassion from it that could not be simulated by a member of the evil priesthood. She decided she had to take a risk and find out more about these beings.

In her mind she said, "I know you are different and are part of a group that is moving throughout this marketplace. I am a friend and want to know why you are here." She figured that if they were as evolved as they appeared to be they could read her mind.

Out loud the being said, "My name is Kamur, and this is one of my friends, Questur. We are visiting your fine city. We would appreciate it if you could show us about."

She knew she was taking a chance and would, therefore, involve no one else. Carefully guarding her thoughts, she led them to a small knoll with a large tree and some benches. In a low voice she said,

"I know if I communicate with one of you, I will communicate with all of you. Have you traveled a very great distance to visit?"

Kamur smiled in a knowing way and answered, "Yes, we all have traveled a very great distance. You, too, appear not to be a native of this place."

This could be a trap for her and she had to be wary.

"I, too, came from far away, but I have been at the nearby Temple since I was a child. It has been a wonderful environment for me. I never felt at home before then."

"Yes, I can understand that," replied Kamur. "We also are having difficulty adjusting to this area. It is quite different from our homeland."

"Why have you come to our city?" Shature replied, still disguising what she was really saying. However, Kamur seemed to follow her completely.

"We have come to meet with some friends of ours who have been here quite a while, but with whom we have lost all contact. We were concerned and came in search of them. I wonder if perhaps you have seen them."

"No," she replied. "I have never seen anyone with your qualities before. I'm sure I would have noticed. However, my life is somewhat sheltered at the Temple. I would only have seen them there or in this marketplace. I will ask around for you. Perhaps we can meet again next week at this time and I can tell you what I have discovered."

"We will be here," replied Kamur. He then nodded goodbye, as did his companion, and left.

At that moment, one by one, the other small groups finished their business and moved away from the marketplace. They all went in different directions, but she knew they would meet later with Kamur. She believed their group departure as an act of trust for her and as an affirmation of her suspicions that they were together. She would talk to Ramor about this as soon as possible.

"How could you have taken such a risk?" She had never seen Ramor angry before. His aura was filled with red flashes.

"Please, Ramor, do not be angry. I was very careful. I told them nothing. You underestimate me and my ability to read others.

Remember, I was chosen for this job. You have not seen me much since my initiation. I can understand your worry, but you must trust me more."

Her calm and confident voice soothed him. He was surprised by his unexpected outburst of emotion. He cared for her more than he had realized. Should he tell her or would that be inappropriate?

"I am sorry for my outburst," he followed. "But I truly care for your safety, perhaps more than I realized."

Shature was flattered.

"Thank you for your concern. I know that my job is dangerous, but I must not avoid it. I am confident that they are not an enemy. I observed and 'felt' them for a long time, and I believe that they were doing the same with me. As before, I will divulge nothing to them, but I want to meet them again to determine what they are about. You can send someone to observe me. If all goes well this time, we can determine a mutual spot where we can meet again."

"All right," he conceded. "But, do not linger too long in the marketplace. Sell them something and make it look like a business arrangement. If you find them trustworthy, meet them again in three days under the Fountain Rock. We can observe you there and their escape will also be cut off if they are up to something. If they have come from Arcturus, then they will be our allies."

With his final words, she left feeling excitement and a tinge of fear. In five more days she would meet them. She had a lot of planning to do in the meantime.

The days of waiting sped by. It was now dawn before she went to the marketplace. She was dressed and ready to leave. First, however, she would check inside with her Inner Guide. The blazing golden light of her initiation visited her again and again in her dreams and meditations. Even though her initiation had revealed the golden light as a higher portion of herself, she could not yet totally accept the power of that concept. Instead, she identified the light as an Inner Guide, a being inside herself but separate at the same time. Over time, she had gained a relationship with it and learned to allow its great love to enter her heart. She now trusted it completely. She would need it today to keep her honest with herself. Excitement or strong emotions could blur her vision and she might miss something important without a constant communication with her Guide.

She sat in the corner of her room looking out towards the valley. She lit the wick of the scented oil bowl and closed her eyes to go inside. Almost at once she felt the familiar, loving presence. She had many questions to ask, but she had learned that it was always fully aware of her circumstances and knew her questions before she could ask them. She waited, staring into its luminous eyes and losing herself in its essence. Gradually she began to hear its voice.

"Listen. Listen very carefully. Your personal mission is in danger. These beings are indeed as pure as they appear, but you must proceed with caution. A higher portion of yourself has already determined your destiny and it is imperative that you listen to your own inner prompting. Do not be alone with these visitors, for although they mean well, they could lead you away from your higher purpose."

"Should I abort this meeting?"

"No, there is something which you will gain from this meeting. It is within your path to follow up on your plans, but be cautious. Danger is also an opportunity for growth, both for you and for those whom you wish to help."

With these final words, the presence faded. Shature had learned that once it left, it was finished communicating and there was no point in trying to re-connect. It was time for her to go and she was frightened and surprised. She had not thought of the destiny of which her Guide spoke. She was so sure of herself, so sure of her well-loved instincts. Had her ego been interfering with her ability to perceive the truth? Perhaps she had been wrong about her guidance. Maybe she was not clear about anything and was only imagining everything. For a moment she even doubted her meditation, but she quickly stopped that because she knew that that behavior would surely lead to her destruction.

Everywhere there were conflicting messages. If she couldn't believe the ones which came from deep inside her, then she knew she had no chance for survival. She gathered her things and headed towards the marketplace with her companions. It was just after dawn and the air was filled with mist. She had always loved this time of day—sunrise and sunset—times—of transition from one environment, one state of mind, to the next.

When Shature and her companions arrived at the market place, they discussed their plans while they awaited their meeting. Her companions were there to watch over her. Just before the sun had risen a quarter of the way in the sky, like last week, the visitors arrived and made themselves look busy unpacking cases.

Shature and one of her friends approached the visitors carrying boxes which they would 'trade' with the mysterious strangers. She could feel the warmth of their essence long before she was physically close to them. She must be careful to guard her thoughts since they were very good at reading them.

"Hello," she welcomed them. "We have brought herbs and spices grown in our gardens at the Temple."

"Thank you," replied their leader. "We have also brought what you have asked for, jewelry made of shells and minerals from our homeland."

As she looked at the jewelry, she saw that it was made of materials not available on Earth. She tuned into his thoughts to see if he had an explanation. What she received was:

"You were right. We are from another planet. You must trust us. We mean you no harm. This area is in great danger, and unless this danger is addressed, it can destroy the entire planet. We only wish to assist you."

"How helpful of you," she replied out loud. "You know how needful of it we are."

He smiled at her and replied, also verbally,

"We would like to show you what else we can do for you. If you could follow us to our camp, we can talk in depth about our transaction."

Shature, remembering Ramor's warning politely declined.

"I am sorry, we are too busy now, but we will return in three days and meet you in the valley just south of here under the large rock. It is known as Fountain Rock. Trust must be built slowly for both of us!" Shature said as she looked sternly into his eyes.

"We will be there!"

As they were returning to the Temple, she reflected on their meeting. She had much to say to Ramor. She had not had time to tell him of her morning meditation. She felt frightened, confused and excited. What did all this mean and what should she do next? She decided to go inside herself before she met with Ramor. She had difficulty at first, as she had so many conflicting emotions, but at lest she felt connected.

"You did fine today," spoke Shature's inner guide. "Continue the communication with these beings. But proceed very slowly. Meet with them as planned, but inform Jatain and bring him with you. He also has a role to play here."

Jatain was more than ready for the challenge and excitement. Ramor agreed to the plan but was very cautious.

"Be careful. They could be followed by the dark forces," cautioned Ramor. "They have been reported observing the visitors as well."

Shature went inside herself again for further instruction, but received none. She would have to follow through on her plans and stay alert. She felt much safer with Jatain there. Her relationship with him had continued to grow and they were, in fact, talking about naming a date for their bonding.

The visitors returned three days later at the Fountain Rock. However, Shature, Jatain and the others had waited many hours with no sign of the strangers. Just as they were preparing to leave, the visitors arrived.

"We could not come sooner. We believe we were being observed. We cannot meet like this again. Can we come to your temple as soon as it is safe for us? We know where it is."

Shature looked at Jatain. His look transmitted to her,

"If they know where it is, what harm can it do?"

"Please come to our garden on the south side of the Temple at your convenience and we will communicate again. Have you found your companions yet?"

"No, we have not found them. We will meet you again soon," he replied hurriedly. He looked over his right shoulder in a worried fashion and quickly left, heading north.

"He looked almost frightened," noticed Jatain.

"Yes, and I think he was keeping something from us. I wonder where the others are? I don't sense them anywhere near this area."

"We will slowly gather our things while we observe the area. Then all we can do is go back," replied Jatain. "Do you think we should try to follow them?"

"We can't now that we have lost sight of him. Also, my inner instructions were clear to not be alone with them. We will meet them on our own territory."

Many days passed without seeing them. It was almost a month before they arrived at the garden. All of them were together, except for one, but something was different. They didn't seem to have as much vitality and their auras had streaks of gray in them. Shature's first instinct was that they had been sick.

"Are you well?" She greeted them.

"Your planet is not comfortable for us. There are many dark vibrations and we have become ill from the constant effort of fending them off. We have decided to go home. We cannot stay here long enough to help."

"Have you been followed by the dark forces?" asked Jatain.

"No, we were very careful. We would not do anything to endanger you. We have come to help, but we cannot survive here. One of us has expired and we believe that is the fate of our other companions. We are representatives of a Universal Order. We are here to determine if your planet can prevent the impending disaster and we have determined that it cannot. We do not believe that there will be much left after the final cataclysm. However, if there are survivors, we will return with more representatives to assist in the reconstruction."

Jatain responded. "We are also aware of the dangers here and have reached the same conclusions. We will work to save those we

55

can and to establish safe points for those who have been chosen to carry on. There are many who will not listen and who will even silence those who dare to speak the truth. Perhaps you could still be of assistance if you could provide a route of escape if none other is available.

"At the time of the cataclysm, some of us will pass over with the masses to assist them in their fearful deaths. Others will immigrate to new safe areas while there is still time. However, there are also the dark forces that need a place to hide. A different planetary existence would not be difficult for them. Perhaps an exchange of information would be of benefit to all concerned."

The leader of the foreign emissaries smiled and replied,

"Yes, we were going to make that offer ourselves. Yanour here," said Kamur while pointing to one of the healthiest looking members of the group, "has made the best adaptation to your environment and is willing to stay as a permanent emissary. He can contact us when necessary and inform us of any way in which we can be of help to you. In exchange, we would like for one of you to go with us."

Shature's heart sank. She knew that Jatain was the one who was best suited for this task. The thought of losing another love was more than she could take and her eyes filled involuntarily with tears. Jatain knew her emotions and replied to the leader.

"We must confer upon this. Can you spend the night here while arrangements are made?"

"No, we must return, but we will be back here in twenty-four of your hours."

With this, the entire group turned and left. Shature's heart had sunk to her stomach and she could not lift her eyes from the ground. She felt Jatain's gentle touch as he led her back inside the Temple.

"NO!" she cried. "I will not allow it. How many sacrifices must I make?"

Jatain was calm and looked into her face with such love and gentleness that she knew she could not change his mind.

"We are here for a greater purpose," he calmly reminded her. "We cannot allow our personal lives to endanger our higher purpose. I have waited for my call and we both know that this is it. There is no one better qualified than I am. I have known the situation almost from the beginning and I am very adaptable in new environments. I am a part of this plan."

She felt a rage well up in her, not towards Jatain but towards that inner guidance which always seemed to guide her straight into the jaws of pain. Was this her higher purpose? To be alone again? But she knew Jatain was right, and she would not ruin his moment with her fear and anger. If he stayed for her, he would become less than himself and grow to hate her for it. She had no choice. If she had to let him go, she would do so with dignity.

"I can't watch you go. Stay with me this evening, and in the morning we will say goodbye. We have almost twenty-four hours, so let us make enough memories to last the rest of our lives."

He embraced her in love and gratitude while she struggled to push all of her negative emotions to the back of her mind. She would have plenty of time to review them after he was gone.

They made the most of their final hours together. They walked in their favorite woods, swam in their favorite pond, and watched the sunset from their favorite cliff. In every one of these places they made love—desperate, passionate, and yet, tender love. When, at last, they went to bed, they made love again and again. She took no precautions. She didn't care. Perhaps he would leave a small portion of himself with her. It was well past dawn, their usual hour of awakening, when he looked at her with eyes that said,

"I must leave now."

So soon? She wanted to say. But she would keep her promise with herself. He had arrangements to make. He was starting an entirely new life. He needed this time alone. He dressed, and when he was ready to leave, she pulled herself out of bed and wrapped herself in her robe.

"Somehow I will return to you," he promised.

She wanted to believe him, but she couldn't. She feared she might never see him again, at least, not in this life. She pushed that thought from her mind and embraced him with every essence of her being. He kissed her, long and lovingly, then turned and left the room. As soon as the door closed behind him, she fell to the floor, unconscious. She did not awaken until he had left the planet. Somehow she knew that if she had been able to, she would have tried to stop him.

The weeks that followed were filled with dull pain and grieving. She threw herself into her work and allowed herself no time to reflect or linger on her deep anguish. She also found no time to meditate. She acted as if she were fine. In fact, everyone was proud of how well she was accepting her loss. But, inside she was angry-- angry at her guidance and angry at her destiny. She had enough presence of mind to know that this anger was dangerous. Yet she didn't care and the anger grew like a fire, covered once with a thin layer of sand, waiting for the slightest breeze to set it into a blaze.

However, as the days turned into weeks and the weeks passed into months, she realized that she was no longer alone. She was pregnant. Now she knew she had to heal the anger. Two people were living inside her body and she no longer had the right to harbor and nurture her anger. As she realized this, she felt as if she had just awakened from a dream. She was shocked at what a stranger she had become to herself. She knew it was time to go inside again.

At first she was embarrassed. She had blamed her inner guidance in an attempt to alleviate some of her pain. All it had done was affect her health. Her healer told her that she would have to stay in bed for a least a month or she would lose the baby. She knew it was her anger. How could another being bear the weight of her awful rage? She had to ask for forgiveness. She had volunteered to come to Earth from Venus, but while living in an earthly body, she had lost the higher consciousness which was natural on Venus. Only when she communicated with her inner guide did she experience that feeling of unconditional love and acceptance. She had to return to that feeling in order to keep the baby in her body. It was to be a child of love-- emotional and passionate. It would be a special child. She would have to put aside all of her personal feelings and work at creating a psychic environment which was harmonious with its Soul.

For days and days she tried to go inside, but all she could get was a glimpse of her Guide. At last she received a brief message. She had to communicate with the alien who was here in Jatain's place. She had avoided him all this time as if it were his fault. She owed him amends. She had to summon him since she was confined to her bed. When he arrived at her doorway, she was ready. She offered him some tea, which he accepted, and they stared at their cups as they drank. Finally, they both started to speak at once.

She raised her hand and said,

"Please, let me begin. I owe you an apology. It was my responsibility to make you feel welcome, but I have been so angry at the loss of my loved one that I have avoided you instead."

"I know," he answered. "I could see in your auras that you loved one another. You both have made a great sacrifice for a higher purpose, but soon our communications will be established and you can talk to him."

That thought made her excited and, strangely, afraid. She realized that it was almost easier to leave him completely out of her life, rather than far, far away and just beyond her grasp.

Yanour instantly understood her thoughts and replied,

"He shall return. I also wish to return to my home. This is a temporary exchange."

"Yes, I know that is the plan, but I must admit that I fear otherwise. Please excuse me. I do not mean to frighten you. My concerns are for Jatain, not you. I am constantly worrying that something will happen to him. Perhaps that is a normal reaction to the departure of a loved one," she tried to reassure herself. "But please, let us talk about you. I am sorry to summon you, but I am with child and am presently confined to my bed. In fact, that is the reason why I have come to my senses and realized that I must communicate with you. How are you doing here? I have abandoned you since you have been with us."

"It has been an adjustment, but I have made several friends. I anxiously await communication with my people. In a few days, I believe that will be possible. The dark forces on your planet have made it necessary for us to create a secret line of communication that they cannot monitor. I will let you know as soon as it is in operation. Being unable to communicate all this time has made me also feel very alone. However, I have found your environment here in the Temple similar to that of our traveling vessel.

"I have spent most of my life on that vessel, which is why I volunteered for this assignment. Being on a planet rather than moving through space is what I desire most at this time. Also, it is a new adventure."

Shature smiled.

"Yes, adventure. Often it does turn out quite differently than we expect."

They talked warmly for some time and parted with a sense of camaraderie. He agreed to tell her as soon as communications were arranged. As he left her room, she settled down into her bed and fell into the deepest sleep that she had experienced since Jatain left.

In her dreams that night, Shature again found herself on the cliff reliving the first entry into her body. However, this time the form was more familiar and not as foreign. She re-experienced the separation from her other half and again felt the intense fear and sense of loss. This fear was like a dusty gas that suffocated her and drove her Complement away from her. She had made this fear an enemy in much the same way that she had alienated Yanour. She would have to make friends with this fear as she had made friends with Yanour. Shature must learn to accept, communicate with, and understand how she had created her fear.

In her dream, she began moving into the fear. It was like a dense fog all around her, and she could see nothing. Shature had to remember to control her breath because she was terrified. She had to find her way through the fog in order to...to what? She did not know. In desperation, she called inside herself and saw a light--very dim and far in the distance. At least she had a point of focus now. Shature moved toward the light and it appeared to also move toward her. Finally, with all her force of will, she moved her arm through the dense fog and touched the light. As she touched the light, the fog disappeared. Shature then found herself face to face with herself — her other half.

She awakened suddenly. She understood now. It was her fear that had created her sense of separation. Fear had separated her from her Complement and only love could make her whole. With that thought, she fell back into a dreamless sleep and did not awaken until the next morning.

As the dawn struck her face, Shature remembered. She remembered her dream, she remembered Venus, and she, most of all, remembered Lamire. She had finally united with him, with herself. She was finally whole. However, half of her was not here in the physical world, but rather existed in the spiritual worlds. In between was a bridge with all the colors of the rainbow and all the tones of the scale. Shature would learn to use that bridge, constantly and with every breath. She would learn to live consciously in the awareness that she was One. Shature would allow the peace of that realization to fill her consciousness, just as it had on Venus.

And now, she just had to remember to remember!

CHAPTER THREE

The Bridge

The next fifteen years passed in a moment. Shature communicated with Jatain often, but she saw him only once in the first seven years when he returned for their son's seventh birthday to participate in the naming. Their son was named Vidann, which meant "the builder," because his life reading predicted that he would have a large part in the reconstruction after the great change. Shature had wished that Jatain could have attended their son's birth, but it hadn't been safe for him to return at that time. Again, Shature had stood alone.

Birth on Venus was quite different from birth on Earth. For one thing, the Venusian parents would know the soul that was to inhabit their child. When a being determined that the body was worn out or that it needed a rest, they would pick parents for their next incarnation. They would then walk into the Flame of Life for transmutation. The Flame of Life was actually a vortex that could carry the soul either home to the higher dimensions or back to the

65

fifth dimension for incarnation. It was called the Flame because it appeared to be a large violet flame that was surrounded by the Violet Temple. Once a person chose to enter the Flame from their fifth dimensional home on Venus, the Flame would take up the atoms of the old form and reconstruct them into a new shape.

When it was time for the soul to again embody, the chosen parents would reach into the Flame together and bring forth the life spark of the child. This spark was a miniature adult, but with little life force. The couple would nurture this seed of life spark with unconditional love and their own life force until the body was strong enough for the soul to re-enter it. After that, the child reached adulthood quickly and remembered his former life and everyone from it. Death did not involve forgetting, but was more like sleep. It was a time for the soul to return to the Spirit World for rejuvenation and further instruction.

Shature learned from her labor that human birth was quite different. She was unprepared for the helplessness of her infant, but she found the process of bonding and mothering wonderful. It was through her experience of mothering that she finally came to peace with her physical body. When Vidann was two years of age, he was secure enough to be left with others during the times that she carried out her many duties at the Temple. There was much to do. The time of change would be coming soon. Already, there were more and more earthquakes. Those who had aligned themselves with the dark side were so attached to their personal power that they would not accept change, even in the face of total destruction. They continued to rule as they had always done, no matter what the cost to others and themselves. They had lived in lies so long that they refused to face the truth. They continued to overuse their power sources and to pollute the Earth with waste materials. They continued their Black Magic because it worked best and quickest for them, and they ignored how its low vibration affected the stability of the planet. There were also the dangerous and evil beings whom the dark forces had created. These "un-humans" were the lost ones who lingered in the and were urged into form by the rituals of Black Magic. They had no soul and made perfect slaves for their creators. They terrified the people and even turned on their masters. Now the members of the Temple hardly dared to leave its grounds, as the cities and even the countryside were full of these roving demons.

For the past several years, Shature had been so busy with her work that she had not had a chance to think of herself. After the child's seventh birthday, Jatain had been able to return to the Temple on a regular basis to be with her and Vidann. She had also developed a warm and intimate relationship with Yanour, who was like an uncle to her son. Ramor was like Vidann's grandfather, and a father and mentor to her. Through all of the years and all of her problems, Ramor had been a constant part of her life. His calm strength served as a beacon to guide her through her emotional crises. Finally, after all these years of mothering, service, and intimate friendships, she had grounded herself in her human form. The entry had been long and slow. On Venus, the neural patterning of the brain was such that it had evolved beyond the emotional irrationality of the human brain. Her greatest human challenge had been to learn how to prevent herself from falling into the caldron of emotions that awaited deep inside her earthly brain.

As she continued to master her emotions, it was easier to learn to control her thoughts. Thoughts wanted to come upon her uninvited, and she had to learn to command them into obedience. She was the one who was in control of her. She was not her thoughts, her emotions, or even her body. She was a being of Light. She was a Venusian. She had to remember who she was in order to stay in control of her physical body. Her intense emotions had been in control because she was not fully in her form. The animal, which was the form, would then become unruly and undisciplined and have its way with her.

Shature now understood that fear was the emotion that initiated most of her problems. When she allowed herself to fall into her fear, she would recoil from her human form and leave her physical self in command of her spirit. However, if she denied her fear, it became a hidden enemy that struck when she was least prepared. With discipline, meditation, and patience she gained the ability to recognize her fear and acknowledge it without becoming its victim. If she could remember that she was a Venusian on Earth on a mission of love and mercy, she could calm the fear that welled up within the depths of her humanness. When she placed her consciousness in her Higher Self and higher purpose, she could comfort her lower form. In all of her agony of being abandoned, she had actually abandoned her self, her mission, and her very reason for existence. If she could keep a connection with her Venusian consciousness, she could stay in mastery of her physical vehicle and her destiny.

By Vidann's fifteenth birthday, everyone in her group knew that Atlantis would soon be destroyed. Shature and Yanour had worked with Jatain and the Arcturians to establish an escape route for those who were in danger of being found out by the dark forces. They had also established the location of safe areas where groups could be sent to begin a new life. The work of the hundred and forty four thousand was almost complete. There were few remaining who would hear the truth even though many people still inhabited the continent of Atlantis. The ones who would face the truth had immigrated to other areas or were giving service until the end. It was time for the final exodus to safer locations. Yanour had returned to his people and Jatain had returned to Earth to take Shature and their son to safety. However, as soon as she began to plan for her departure, the dreams of the great flood returned.

Night after night she awoke in terror seeing the waters bursting through the walls of her room. This was not how it was supposed to be. Jatain was taking Vidann and her to safety. Why, then, was she being prepared for this lonely and terrifying death? She tried to communicate with her inner guide, whom she now could recognize as her Higher Self, but every time she tried, a fear would well up within her and the communication would be terminated. She finally realized that she would have to enter the dream awake and face her fear!

She knelt before the wall that she had seen many times in her dreams, closed her eyes and awaited the vision of the oncoming waters. She felt the terror rise up in her and focused on a small spec of light before her inner eye. She was a Venusian. She was a being of Light. She had volunteered for this assignment. If it was her destiny to die here, then she would accept it. With that thought, she saw Lamire, her Complement, before her as a glowing, golden being of light. He came to her and held her in a warm embrace of deep love and acceptance. During that moment she knew that she could face anything. She was not alone. She was One. In the many years that she had worked so hard to ground herself in the Earth, he had worked to ground himself in the higher dimensions of Light. When they joined in that moment, they connected a circuit of pure cosmic force that could be channeled through her into the core of the Earth.

The Earth needed that circuit to stay on its axis at the moment of the cataclysm. As she felt the current move through her, she was aware of all the others who had knowingly or unknowingly volunteered to be a channel of Cosmic Light to assist the Earth in her moment of challenge. In her vision, she saw the waters breaking through the stone wall before her. She felt a surge of fear and heard the joint voices of she and Lamire say,

"I AM that I AM

I AM in service to the Father Mother God.

I give of this life freely and lovingly so that the planet may survive."

As they chanted this decree, Shature felt the deepest, purest and most unconditional Love she had ever known. This love came from the higher dimensions and flowed through the joint circuitry that she and her Divine Complement had created to ground the love in the planet Earth. Shature was ready.

When she awoke from her vision, she knew it was time to send Jatain and her son away with the others whose destiny it was to relocate. She would tell them all that the time was now. They must leave, but she must stay. Life was not physical, but spiritual, and it would never end. It would only change!

The awareness of this truth had been very disturbing and also very illuminating. As soon as she had calmed herself, she knew that she must first go to her beloved Ramor to tell him. When she had told him of her vision, he looked deeply into her and said,

"Yes, I must also stay, and there are two others. Interestingly, our rooms are at the four corners of the temple, as if this had been the plan from the very beginning. Over the years, this temple has become a vortex of energy and now it shall be used for its true purpose."

"Do the others know yet?" asked Shature.

"If they do, they haven't told me. In fact, I don't even know if they are aware of their Complements yet. If they do not make their connections in time, we will have to do the ceremony alone."

"But can't we tell them?"

"No, they must discover the truth for themselves."

"I understand. I am telling Jatain and our son to leave with today's tide on the Temple's last remaining sea ship. I fear the time is very near. Is there anyone else I should warn?"

"No, there are only a few, and I will tell them. You take all the time you need to say goodbye, again, to your loved ones."

She smiled. Goodbye was a word with which she was familiar and had finally learned not to fear. She kissed Ramor on the forehead as she left and was surprised to find not fear in her heart, but joy.

She told Jatain and Vidann that they must leave that day, to pack only what they needed, and to meet her on the dock just before tide. They would sail with the evening tide. She could have given herself more time with them, but she realized that that could have been more difficult. There were only a few hours, and she needed to go within again and spend time in communication with Lamire. They had to bond completely, unifying physical and spiritual. Finally, she had learned to put her personal self second to her divine mission.

When she returned from her contemplation, she knew that it was time to go to the dock. She gathered up a few things to give Jatain and Vidann by which to remember her. For her son, she packed the statue of Varnika, The Venusian Great Mother. And for Jatain, she gathered her life's writings and wrote a small message to him:

My Beloved,
    For all the life
        I have not shared with you,
            look within these pages.
                Our Love Lives!
                    -- SHATURE

Shature had finished packing and was heading through the door when she understood why she had not spent the day with her family, but instead, in deep meditation. She realized that choosing to leave was just as difficult as being left.

When she arrived at the dock, they were waiting. Vidann was as tall as she now and almost a man. To her surprise, after their long embrace he held her at arm's length and looking straight into her eyes, said, "You aren't coming with us, are you Mother?"

"How did you know?"

"It is a dream I had many, many times as a child. Standing here with an unknown man, whom I now know as my father, knowing that you would leave us. It used to frighten me, but over the years it grew to become almost comforting."

"But dear, why did you never tell me of it?"

"My inner guide told me not to. He said it was a gift for me alone, and that one day I would be able to tell you, but I must wait. Now I understand."

"Do you know why I must stay?"

"Not really, but I accept it. Just as father had to leave before I was born, I must be parted from you when I am almost an adult. Sometimes our destiny is more important than our personal loves."

With tears in her eyes, and deep love in her heart, she embraced him for the final time. He had become a man and a very wise one indeed! She gave him her gift and turned to Jatain. No words were necessary or spoken. They held each other long and hard and then looked into each other's eyes in a final unspoken goodbye. She gave him her gift and turned to walk away. That first step away from them was the most difficult thing she had ever done, even more difficult than her entry into an Earth body. She dared not look back as her steps turned into a run. She had to create as much distance from them as possible. When she reached the temple, she shut the door behind her and ran to the balcony to watch their ship leave port. Only from this safe distance could she see them leave forever!

Jatain and Vidann watched Shature's shape grow smaller and smaller. As they sailed away from Atlantis, Jatain put his arm around his son's shoulders and said,

"I realize now that I also have had a recurring dream. I was viewing the temple as it grew smaller and smaller. I kept thinking that I had forgotten something or someone in it, and I wanted to go back and get it. But it was too late. Now I, too, understand my dream. Our Guides have told us of this moment. It has been fated for a very long time, and we are just now carrying it out. We have much work to do, my son. We will carry your mother in our hearts while we do it."

As the sun began to set, so did a major chapter in their lives. The old life must die and be released, like the old skin of a snake, so that the new one could become fully manifest. All that was known moved farther and farther away. As they turned to go into their cabin, they knew they were beginning a new adventure.

That evening when Shature was in the dining room, she looked around at those who were left, wondering which two were destined to hold the other corners of Light. Since she was female and Ramor was male, she assumed that the other two were also male and female. She made a mental note of which of those remaining had rooms in the corners of the temple and came up with only four possible candidates--three women and one man. If her male-female theory was correct, than Vicor had to be the man and one of the three other women was to act as the fourth pillar of Light. She looked into their auras to see if she could see anything unusual, but everyone was already under such a challenge, knowing the true danger of their circumstances, that it was impossible to read anything specific. It was not her concern, she told herself. Each person must make their own choices about whether or not they would embrace their destiny. But, still, she could not resist the temptation to go over to Vicor and engage him in conversation.

At first he said nothing that would lead her to believe that he was aware of his assignment, if indeed it was his, but then perhaps he was sheltering her as she had been sheltering him. A more direct approach may be necessary. She decided to tell him about leaving her son and Jatain, partially to lead the conversation in the correct direction. And honestly, she also needed to talk about it. Vicor had been a dear friend for many years. There was such sympathy and understanding on his face that she was sure he knew he was staying.

Without thinking, she blurted out, "How do you feel about this assignment?"

She knew at once by the look of confusion on his face that she had made a mistake. She had frightened him because she was afraid, and she felt horrible. She tried to cover up her mistake with a rambling sentence to allow him an excuse not to answer her. Finally, she gave a polite reason why she had to return to her room and left him behind her. She had been wrong. She was trying to force someone else into a realization that might be premature or even incorrect. When she reached her room, all the sadness of losing her loved ones once and for all, together with the fear of facing death, overwhelmed her. She collapsed on to her bed and wept.

Somehow, in the midst of her emotion, she felt a strong touch on her shoulder. When she turned around, she saw nothing. But, when she again felt the force of her emotions, she felt the touch. This time it was even firmer. She turned, and again there was nothing. She dried her eyes and sat up on her bed. She had the feeling that she was not alone, but she still could see nothing.

"Open your inner eyes," she heard from within herself.

She closed her physical eyes and attuned herself to her inner vision. Before her was her Higher Self.

"Was that you? I felt you like you were physical," she spoke with her mind.

"Yes, my One, I am physical through you. In passing this most difficult of initiations, you have expanded your consciousness so greatly that you could even *feel* my touch."

"But I was crying. How could my consciousness be aware when I allowed myself to fall into such a state?"

"My One, your state, as you put it, is a healthy and normal reaction to your circumstances. You still live in a physical vehicle and therefore have to respect its needs. To deny yourself the truth of your emotions would be more damaging to your consciousness than to allow yourself to experience them-- briefly. However, I did interrupt you so that you would not get lost."

Shature's meditation was suddenly interrupted by a knock at her door.

"You must answer the door," continued the golden being. "Remember, I am you -- Complete."

She stood up, feeling the power of her spiritual connection. It was Vicor.

"May I come in?"

"Of course."

She led him to a small table and chairs in her room and started to make him some tea.

"No, please," he said. "No formalities are needed. Could you just sit down here for a moment?"

She sat down across from him and he began to speak,

"I owe you an apology. No, please do not respond yet." He reached across the table and held her hand as she tried to interrupt him.

"My reaction to your question needs an explanation. I was shocked and confused, but not for the reason that you probably think. I, too, am aware of our 'assignment', as you so tactfully put it. My reaction was not to our task, but to another issue. You see, I also knew there were four of us. But I didn't know who all of them were. I knew it was Ramor, Lateen and myself. In my selfishness, I assumed, or rather hoped, that the fourth person was my mate. When I realized that the fourth person was you, I knew that I too would have to send my beloved away.

"I am a very selfish person. I actually wished for her to stay so that I wouldn't have the pain of sending her away. I so wanted her to be the fourth person that I assumed she just hadn't found out yet. In realizing that you were the fourth person, I was so overcome with a myriad of emotions that I could not respond at all. Please understand it is not that I am disappointed that it is you. We have been good friends for many years. I was only thinking of my own selfish needs. I see now that the One has set this up for me as a final initiation to purify me for the event."

"I understand, Vicor. I thought I would die when I turned and left Jatain and Vidann on the dock. I ran all the way to the temple for fear I would lose my conviction. I could only watch them leave when I was safely on the highest balcony."

Vicor gently stroked Shature's hand that he just now realized he had been holding.

"Thank you for being so understanding. Did you know that the other woman was Lateen?"

"No, I did not. Did you?"

"Yes, after the last sea ship left I received a message that it was Lateen and me, but I only knew it was also Ramor when I went to him to share my news."

"Does Lateen know?" Shature asked.

"I don't know. She has said nothing if she does. I received that it was Lateen at the same time that I realized I was to stay. I do not know why. Perhaps by knowing two others, it would force me into the very situation that happened today. Thank you again for being so understanding. I must make preparations for my mate to leave now and try to explain to her what I have done."

They stood and embraced each other. As he turned to leave he said,

"We will likely be seeing a great deal of each other in the future."

It seemed like all of Lateen's life she had felt unworthy, not good enough, and worst of all, alone. Her friendship with Shature had waned after Jatain entered Shature's life, and Lateen knew that she felt so alone because no one loved her. She remembered the loss of her Complement and missed her talks with Shature about being androgynous. When Shature created her new life, Lateen felt as though the only one she could talk to was gone, except of course her Complement, whom she could not reach. She searched for him everywhere -- in all her meetings, in her everyday life, in her meditations, and in her dreams. Still, he was totally elusive. Once in a while she would catch a glimmer in the corner of her eye or a slight flicker of light in her meditations. Then there was the presence in her dreams. It took on many different shapes and roles in her dream life, but there was a consistent familiarity that continued to reappear.

Perhaps this presence was her Complement, and she just could not recognize him.

Also, there was "the memory". She had titled it that because it was a recurring picture in her mind. She was standing among a very large group of people listening to someone speak. But the people were different, and so was she. She was one of them, and they were from someplace else, far, far away. Shature had helped her remember that the place was Venus and that the person speaking was the High Chancellor. Lateen loved "the memory", and welcomed it whenever it came to her mind, because it was the only time that she truly felt she at peace. Recently the memory had become almost a constant companion and she was regaining more and more recollection of her life on Venus. She knew that she had come to Earth to assist, but she could not find her place. She was not a natural leader like Vicor, nor was she as psychic as Shature. She felt as though she was on the edge of Temple activity, and sometimes on the edge of life itself. The only time she truly felt alive was in her meditations, which were many.

Lateen's meditations were now beginning to bring her a deep understanding. A Golden Light had entered her meditation and told her that she had been chosen to stay. She had no idea what those words meant, but if this Golden Light chose her then she would surely obey its request. She knew that staying would mean her physical death, but that did not dismay her. She felt only half alive in this physical world, and death meant that her physical self could join the greater part of her that had been waiting for as long as she could remember. After the Golden Light came to her, her dream person came more often to tell her about life on Venus. It appeared to be a male and felt familiar, but he was as illusive as ever. Lateen tried and tried to join him, but something always stopped her. The pain of being so close and yet so far was overwhelming. Lateen became morose and kept to herself even more than before. She talked to no one and barely left her room except to go to the garden, wander among the trees, or teach the children music. Lateen was almost constantly in meditation, but it seemed that the harder she tried to connect with her dream messenger, the more difficult it became. She was certain she was on the edge of insanity.

Lateen was glad that no one had observed her difficulties. There was such disturbance and upheaval in the Temple with so many people preparing to leave that she was largely ignored. Ignored because no one cared, she told herself as she gardened alone. But, she deserved that. "I have never cared for anyone else so why should they care for me," she thought as she threw her hoe down onto the damp earth. Not even the children cared. She was gardening alone—again. Disgusted with her life and with herself, she stomped off into the surrounding woods. She walked faster and faster, as if to outrun her pain until she was indeed running. She was running as fast as she could. Without any notice that she had crossed the boundaries of the Temple grounds she continued, looking neither to the right nor to the left. So what if she got lost, or worse, captured by one of the evil soulless ones that roamed the hills at night. No one would care! But, even in her own self pity, she heard that thought and took a moment to asses her situation. Yes, Lateen had indeed run far beyond the safety of the Temple's protective aura. She had no idea where she was and, since she found herself in a deep valley, she did not even know which direction to go. Dense clouds covered the sun and, to make matters worse, it was almost dark. Now she had done it. She had brought about what she had feared. She would die alone with no one either knowing or caring about her plight.

Where was that Golden Light now that she needed it so much? "Wait," Lateen calmed herself. How could she meditate when she was in such a rage? She had chosen her life and there was no point in regretting it at this late stage. She sat down on a log and closed her eyes. At first, all she could feel was the evil entities roaming the shadows awaiting her next move. No, she could not fall into her fear now. She had to regain her center and communicate with the Golden Light. Just as Lateen began to calm herself, she heard a loud noise and the rumble of underbrush coming in her direction. She fought the urge to run. Instead, she surrounded herself with the aura of invisibility. She was a Priestess. Her light would protect her. But the noise became louder and louder and her imagination was stronger than her faith as she felt a terror building in her stomach.

"Please, help me!" she called to the light that she could not see but believed in. "I am a Priestess and in need of your protection."

The noise stopped and terror was gradually replaced by a deep, deep love. Lateen could feel the love which emanated from within her heart and also from just in front of her. Could it be, could it be that her Complement had come to her rescue?

"I am always with you," was the reply, "Even if you are unaware of me, I am ALWAYS with you."

Lateen slowly opened her eyes. In the dim light of sunset, she could recognize the face of her Complement. When at last he was there before her, she did not know what to say or do.

"Follow me," he said simply as he turned to lead her back to the Temple.

When, at last, they entered the safety of the Temple grounds, Lateen's Complement turned to face her. They stared into each other's eyes for what seemed to be a lifetime.

"Why have you cut yourself off from me?" he said at last.

"But I have not. I have been trying to join with you, but have not been able to."

"It is true that we are to rejoin into one being again, but you have fallen into your loneliness and isolation. In order for us to become one again, you must confront your fear."

"Which fear? I have many."

"The fear that you have no value. Because of this fear you have isolated yourself from others. Together we are to aid in creating a bridge that can be crossed at the time of the cataclysm. You must anchor your end of it in the physical world. This cannot be done until you have healed your fear of unworthiness."

"But how? How can I feel worthy?"

In response to her question, the woods around her began to blur and the ground and sky seemed not to exist. All that she could see was her Complement. For a moment she became afraid, but his eyes silently comforted her and she relaxed into the experience. She could feel herself gradually transcending all that she had known, and feared, as she floated into and through a land of such pristine beauty that she could hardly contain the many emotions that fought to arise in her.

"Be calm," whispered his eyes. "All this will be yours, as this is your true home."

She had a million questions, but the peace was so overpowering that she could not formulate any of them in her mind. She floated above all questions and allowed herself to absorb the deep state of calm about her.

"You can stay here with me here now or you can return to your physical self to heal your pain and complete our mission."

Return, she thought. Why would she want to do that? She looked into his eyes and felt a gentle understanding and comfort.

"I am your Divine Complement. I have felt the pain of separation, just as you have. In fact, I have felt all your pain and loneliness but have known that we would be united eventually. I am sorry that we could not communicate before now so that you, too, could hold the knowledge."

As her Complement spoke, Lateen found herself considering returning to Earth. She had waited this long, and now she knew that she would eventually rejoin with her complete self.

"You are needed, Lateen. You have been recognized, and it is a great honor to be chosen for this task. However, the choice is yours. If you return, you must heal your fear so that you can ground our essence in the Mother Earth with the joint force of our love. To do that, you must know that you are worthy. I await your answer, my beloved. As you return to your clay form remember me, remember us, as you make your decision."

"But how can I feel worthy?"

"I can tell you no more at this time. You must find that answer for yourself."

The vision disappeared, and Lateen was once again alone in the woods. Her unanswered question echoed in the empty forest. She sat upon a fallen log and contemplated her life on Earth. She had spent so much time alone. What had she gained by that? Had she ever helped anyone? NO! She had only been interested in herself. " STOP!" she screamed inside her mind. Enough of this self pity. If I were without value, I would not have been saved from whatever fate awaited me in the darkness of that lost valley. If I were without value, the Golden Light would not have chosen me to stay and my Complement would not have answered my call. I have been alone because it was my choice, and, perhaps, it was also my destiny. I have judged myself all of my life. And because I thought so poorly of myself, I believed that others shared my opinion. I am a Priestess, not a child. I take responsibility for the life that I have created and choose to believe that I was answering an inner call.

Feeling stronger, Lateen walked back towards the Temple along her familiar route. She remembered how she had fought to keep this forest pure so that the animal's lives would not be disturbed. As she walked along the path that she had created, she saw small groups or individuals meditating or talking beneath the tall trees. If it had not been for her, the trees would have been logged. She looked up and saw the many birds and other creatures living in the trees. Just before she arrived at the Temple was the garden that she had planted and taught the local children to tend. Two youngsters with curly hair dropped their hoes and ran to her side.

"Lateen, are we having our music lesson tonight?"

"Yes, at the same time as always," she said as she patted their heads.

As she entered the Temple, she saw one of the kitchen chefs with his arms full of freshly picked produce.

"Oh, hello Lateen," he waved to her almost dropping the carrots. "I am so grateful for your garden. Since it is no longer safe to go to the marketplace, it is our only source of fresh fruit and vegetables."

"It is not my garden," she called back to him. "It belongs to everyone."

Lateen was beginning to realize that she *had* contributed to those around her.

"Yes," she heard the voice of her Complement from inside of her soul. "You were chosen as one of the four because you have loved Mother Earth and all of Her creations. Perhaps you have not made intimate friends, but in avoiding contact with many adults, you have kept a childlike innocence which allows you to commune with the Earth."

"Yes," agreed Lateen. "I have measured myself against others and fallen short in the comparison. I have created a place for me, but since I could not recognize myself I could not hear the recognition of others. I will stay upon this physical world until it is my destiny to leave. I acknowledge that I have given service because I can now remember that the entire world is One. That which I have given to the smallest of creatures, I have given to all."

Lateen's step seemed lighter as she climbed the stairs to her room. She felt the now constant unity with her Divine Complement as well as with all of life. She would soon return Home, and now she knew that Home was where she had always been.

When Vicor left Shature's room, he did not know what he would say to his mate, but he knew he had to find her and convince her to leave. He realized now how selfish he had been and how he had subtly been convincing her to follow his destiny because he was afraid to face it alone. How could he have been so manipulative, and how could he have been chosen when he had behaved so selfishly? He had to make amends at once, but he did not know how. He knew he would have to find peace within himself before he spoke to his lover. If she saw him in this disturbed state, she would never leave him. She had held herself back in order to care for him, and he now understood that was why she had to be without him as well.

He went to the South Tower that overlooked the ocean. It was here that he spent his time alone in contemplation. As he closed his eyes in order to center himself, he saw the sea rising in a huge wave to overtake the Temple and all the land. He had seen this vision many times, but this time it felt different. He knew that the danger was imminent and that he must act quickly. He struggled to raise his consciousness, but the more he struggled, the more difficult it became to rise above his turmoil. At last he could withstand it no longer. He fell to the ground, sobbing and pounding it like a child. How could he leave her? How could he die?

"Death is but an illusion."

He swung his head around in order to see the bearer of such a pure and sweet voice, but no one was there.

"I am here, my One, deep within you. Now that you have released your selfishness I can communicate with you."

He could not see her, but her voice was like the breeze at dawn. Her warmth and love calmed his heart and he felt totally complete.

"Yes, my beloved. We are complete now. When we took this form, I could not enter. These bodies are polarized and can be only male or female and not complete as we were on Venus. Your Earth brain made you forget me. But your Soul is continuous with mine and reminded you that something was missing. We are together in

Spirit now, and when you have completed your service, we can again be united into one being.

"Your dear mate has her own destiny and has a secret she has also kept from you. She will bring a portion of you with her in your unborn daughter. They shall be priestesses. Go now, my love, they must take the air machine to meet with the sailing ship that carries Shature's family to safety. After you have sent her off, return to this place and I will instruct you further. Go now. I await you!"

He arose in a daze. He knew that with this information he could convince his mate to leave. The pain of losing her could only be eased by the joy of the knowledge of their child. From the higher planes he could oversee her and guide her as he had been guided. As he descended the tower, his heart was full and his face radiant.

In his meditations, Ramor had seen the struggles of Shature, Lateen and Vicor. He knew that he, too, had a sacrifice to make. Since he had entered the body of a High Priest who had worked many years to raise his consciousness, Ramor had been able to maintain a constant connection with his Complement and had always felt her as a physical component of himself. Because Ramor had this great advantage, he had been given many more responsibilities than the others had. The body which he took on was fully adult and self-actualized. Therefore, he did not have to be limited by his relocation, nor did he forget, as did many of the others who took less evolved bodies or who had to enter as infants. Most of these comrades had been identified and were now aware adults. They had done their work and were on their way to various safe areas to assist in starting new societies.

Ramor would not be safe. He was one of the four who was to stay. He now had to experience the separation of the polarities of self that all the others had felt all along. He knew that he had to release his feminine counterpart and have her be his ballast in the spiritual planes so that she could join the Divine Complements of the other three. In this way, there were actually two groups-- one on the physical plane and another on the spiritual plane. It was vital for each of them to have conscious communication with their Divine Complements, who were awaiting them in the spiritual planes to light the path for their ascension. Their Divine Complements would keep them free of fear and negativity, both individually and as a unit. Each Complement was to act as the spiritual end of the bridge upon which the lower self could be guided Home into its own completeness and divinity. Once the four created the bridge, others could cross it as well.

Ramor had felt the separation slowly taking place for several months. Every morning he would awake and feel as though he had forgotten something or someone. Then he would remember with a jolt of pain that he had lost a portion of himself. He felt as though he was slowly and painfully dying. It became increasingly difficult for him to perform his duties, and he looked older and older with every passing day. His health was beginning to fail, and he was constantly fatigued. He realized that the process had to be slow at first, but that now he had to release his feminine self into spirit completely or he may actually die. He knew that he would need help. It was difficult for him to ask, as he had always been the helper, the guide, for others. Now, he needed guidance himself.

With his diminishing awareness, he knew that the other three had accomplished their spiritual connections and were ready for their assignment. He knew they would have to be with him for his final separation or he might not survive. Even now he felt as if a complete and sudden death would be preferable to this slow and tortuous separation. How could he make this sacrifice? What if the cataclysm didn't happen and he was trapped for years and years on this dismal world only half a person?

In a moment of shame, he realized how fortunate he had been. This is how all the others had as throughout their entire time upon this planet. He remembered the terrified child that he had named Shature. She had remembered the separation and had almost died of it. She had lived with that awful pain all these years. He respected Shature deeply now as he truly realized what an agony that had been. He remembered Lateen, whom he had watched develop from a lonely, isolated child into the complete adult that she was today. And Vicor was a young man full of ego and vanity. He had expected everyone to care for him until he came to realize how fully he could care for himself when he achieved his own completeness. Yes, they had all been very brave, and now Ramor would have to match their bravery.

Ramor was concerned for his physical vehicle. It had been alive for many, many years and it had become very old and weak since his separation process had begun. An ever-growing fear had begun to arise in him. Fear was something that he had not known when he was complete, but now it had become his constant enemy. He battled it continuously, and the battle left him tired and angry. He had snapped at everyone lately and had spoken harshly on several occasions. He had to complete this process now, but he realized that his pride was stopping him. He would have to ask for help. The leader would have to be led. The strong would have to be weak. As his Complement receded more and more into the higher dimensions, he began to feel all of the extreme polarities of this physical world. He was frightened and very, very lonely!

Finally, he gathered the courage to call a meeting of the other three. As they all sat in a circle in his altar room, he looked into each one of their faces. It was as if they all knew what he wanted, but also knew that he would have to ask as a part of his process. Finally, he blurted out,

"I need your help. As you evidently know, I now must release my Complement to the higher planes in preparation for our work together. I have watched in admiration as each one of you has found your way. It is very difficult for me to ask for assistance, as I have not had to do so in the past. I can now more deeply appreciate the sacrifice and great achievements of each of you""

"How can we assist you?" spoke Shature. "You know that we will do anything we can."

"I am not sure, myself. I only know that I am weakening every day, more and more. There is a final release that I know I am resisting, and the strain has become very dangerous to my physical vehicle."

"Perhaps if we all go into meditation and call for the assistance of our own Complements, we can facilitate this process on both the inner and the outer planes," suggested Vicor.

They all agreed that this was indeed an excellent idea. As they went into meditation together, the power in the room became almost tangible. The Divine Complements of the three formed a circle of love to beckon Ramor's other half, while the physical bodies of the three surrounded Ramor's and laid their hands upon it to enhance the flow of vital energies into it. Gradually, like stretching a vine to its full length, Ramor's female self receded into the higher spiritual planes. The three massaged Ramor's body from the feet up so that the final separation would take place from the top of the head, and also to nourish and comfort the physical self during this vigorous and dangerous process. Finally, almost with a snap, the process was complete. Ramor was in a deep trance, and they all instinctively knew that he should remain that way for three days and three nights. They moved his body to his sleeping mat and lit candles all around him. At least one of them needed to keep vigil over him at all times.

At the dawning of the third day, they all gathered around him again to call him back to his body. Although he resisted returning, his commitment to his destiny finally led him back into the physical world, while leaving half of himself behind in the higher planes. For a solid week, he remained in his bed while the others fed him and cared for him. His depression was enormous, and he couldn't speak a word for four days. At last on the seventh day, he arose from his mat to face the dawn as he had done for many, many years. This time, however, there were four of them. They met to face the sunrise and sunset together. They also met every day when the sun was straight overhead to share their individual experiences and to prepare for their future task.

Ramor's health gradually returned. In fact, he felt better than ever. Each of them now realized that their Selves extended far beyond their physical form. They were alive and conscious on the spiritual as well as the physical planes. They were like beacons of light that shone with such brilliance from the spiritual planes that they were manifested into form when their light touched the physical world.

The others, who had chosen to stay behind to assist the crossing over of the many who would die, realized that something had happened to these four. They began to come to each of the four with their problems, and mostly with their fears. Those who remained in the Temple were very brave indeed. They knew that they would all die, but they had volunteered to stay behind to assist the many dead and dying at the time of the cataclysm. When so many people die at once in a violent and terrifying manner, the Lower Astral Planes become very turbulent. This turbulence can ricochet back to the Physical Plane and actually make the cataclysm worse. All those who remained realized that none of the continent would survive, but they were hoping to save the planet. If the disaster were too tremendous, the Earth could actually become disengaged from its gravitational field and be spun off into space. As awful as it is for a continent to be destroyed, it is far worse to lose an entire planet.

The earthquakes and tremors were happening more often and becoming more and more severe. Everyone knew that soon the day would come when the entire continent would be destroyed. The people left in the cities, and the forces of darkness that remained on Atlantis, were in denial. Those in power did not wish to lose their positions, so they flatly denied any real danger. There had been many times of geological upheaval. In fact, the continent had grown quite a bit smaller in the last hundred years. The periods of upheaval would eventually end and things would return to normal. Therefore, the dark forces continued with their Black Magic and with the use of the crystal at full power, just as they had always done. The waiting list for the transformer was as long as ever, and all the powerful and wealthy anticipated the addition of several decades to their lives.

However, some of the simple people, especially those who worked with animals or who worked the Earth, began to realize that something was different. These people had very limited resources and no way to leave. The Temple had sent off its last sea ship and air machine. The dark forces and their allied leaders, allowing no means of escape for those who stayed, viciously guarded the few vehicles that remained in the area. More and more of these natural people came to live in or near the Temple. It became as crowded as it had ever been, but now with women, men, children, and animals instead of priests and priestesses. Gradually, everyone in the temple began to partake in the sunrise and sunset ceremonies. Even the children and animals became silent. The members of the darkness and the rich, powerful royalty scoffed at this foolishness and continued their lives as before. The continent was more and more separated into two different elements. The dark and the light became increasingly defined.

The four received, on the next full moon, a message that the end would come! Always, when the moon was full, the configuration of the sun and moon in aspect to the crystal created a stronger energy force than usual. This was a time of special ceremonies, as well as special usage of the crystal. The air machines were fueled and the life regenerators were all run at full speed. The dark forces were also harnessing the increased energy off the crystal for their evil purposes. This full moon would be in Taurus, which was a period of extraordinary power in the physical plane. It had always been a time of special feasting and celebration.

All the members of the Temple were warned, and even the peasants knew that something ominous was about to happen. Everyone could feel the tension in the air. No one left the Temple as the day approached. The dawn ceremony was so charged with power that many people fainted or became ill, and several of the older ones died. Many spent the entire day in meditation.

The four had all said their good-byes to everyone and had retired to their corner rooms to spend the entire twenty-four hour period in contemplation. The Temple was placed at the tip of a peninsula and situated so that each direction had a direct view of the ocean. Shature's room was in the North corner of the Temple, Lateen's was in the East, Vicor's was in the South, and Ramor's room was in the West corner. No thoughts or emotions were allowed by any of the four at this time. They were empty vessels preparing themselves to fulfill their duties.

The first rumbling started as the full moon began to rise, and the Earth was in full turbulence as the moon reached its apex. Each of the four had spent the entire twenty-four hours in deep communion with their Divine Complements. Shature could feel the tension of the Temple threatening to pull her consciousness down, but she chose to focus her attention on her Highest Self. All the pain and loneliness of her life lay below her. It was like crossing a high suspension bridge and looking only at her destination, refusing to acknowledge the treacherous rocks below. As the tremors began, she had to discipline herself greatly to not fall into the fear.

But as the tremors grew, so did her Inner Light. She stared into the blank stone wall before her, and in her mind she saw the waters rushing towards her. She knew that the others were having the same vision. It was the vision they had all seen many times. As she imagined this water, she saw it not as death, but as a reunion with her Lamire, reunion with her spirit and reunion with her destiny. Her physical body was being rocked and buffeted, and she had to tie herself to her altar so that she did not fall about the small room.

Simultaneously, the light became so strong that she was blinded by it. She no longer saw the room around her or even her vision of the wall. The tone was so loud and the light was so brilliant that she no longer heard the quake or even the onrushing waters. She could no longer feel anything. Her emotions had become extinct. Her thoughts were unnecessary. All that was left was this blinding golden light with its accompanying brilliant tone. She stepped into the light as it drew her to its heart. As she took that step, she found she was not alone. Her Complement embraced her, and as she looked around, she saw the other four with their Complements.

They stood in a radiant circle, and within that circle was a vortex of Light that reached below to the troubled Earth. They did not think, nor did they feel. They focused only on balance. Balance to hold the Earth in its gravitational field. They realized at that moment that all over the Earth were other groups of four serving the same purpose. Together they formed a magnetic net of light that protected the Earth from complete destruction. The net was an infusion of their physical and spiritual elements. Spirit and Matter together as one!

From the center of the vortex was a bridge filled with all the colors of the rainbow. Across that bridge came those who believed. Leaving behind their physical forms to the grasps of the onrushing waters, they bravely climbed the bridge to spirit. They left behind the fear and sadness in their empty vehicles because these emotions blurred their vision of the bridge. They pushed aside their anger, at others and at themselves, because it would have trapped them in their dying physical forms. Love alone shone in their hearts and minds. All around the planet, even in areas where the physical vehicle was safe, brave and loving souls realized that this was the closing of an age. In this knowledge they decided to take the opportunity to free themselves from the wheel of birth and death. Since they had faced their darkness and done mortal combat with it, they were able to own their light and see its staircase to a better way.

The Earth would take a long time to recover from this cataclysm, and many courageous souls had chosen to stay behind to help with its reconstruction. But others took this chance to raise their vibrations and continue their existence on the higher planes of reality. Shature and the other three had made the sacrifice to surrender their lives in service to their spiritual destiny. They could choose to reincarnate in a safe area on the planet, serve in the troubled ethers of the Earth, or move into higher planes to continue their evolution. Ramor and Vicor chose to reincarnate, as they believed their leadership qualities would be needed. Vicor was even allowed to enter the yet unborn child of his mate. Ramor reincarnated in Egypt, again to be a Priest. Lateen and Shature chose to stay in the higher planes to continue their evolution.

Shature was sure of her decision as she joined with Lamire above the turbulent ethers surrounding Earth. She was sure of her decision as she embraced him in the cool green fields and clear sky of the higher worlds. She knew that she would be happy and content, or maybe, she hoped it. But she still heard their cries. She still felt their need. Many, many had died in the cataclysm, and most did not even know that they were dead. They kept reliving their horrible death over and over. Because they had not faced their darkness, because they had not embraced their light, they could not see the bridge.

They could not control their fear and sadness that kept their souls in a constant state of upheaval. They also could not control their anger. Therefore, a part of their consciousness was roaming through the ruined memories of their homeland while another part of them relived the deluge again and again. In other words, they were in Hell. She knew that she could help them. Many of them knew her or knew of her. Some of them were evil and cruel, and she would leave them to their fate, since they would not have listened to her anyway. They would rather hold on to the terrifying memory of their lost power than face the humility of their present state.

Some of them, however, were merely led astray. It was a very bad time. These people had no way to see the light because they were surrounded by darkness. They were calling. If someone that she knew was calling for help, how could she turn her back and walk into the fields of glory?

She turned to look into Lamire's eyes. Yes, she saw that he understood. He could go with her now. Their time apart had split them into two separate entities, but because they would not need a physical form in the ethers of Earth, they could be together again, side by side. Would he be willing to go with her? Then she remembered how much it had helped on Earth to know that a component of her complete self was alive on a higher vibration. This higher self often helped her to be objective, to see the true meaning to life's challenges, and to lead her into her destiny. Would she want to give up that higher guidance if she dropped her consciousness into such a troubled environment? No, it would be better if he could assist her from here. She was afraid to return alone, but even more frightened to return to that lower plane without having a beacon in the higher ones.

When Shature was in Atlantis she had learned to raise and lower her vibration in order to enter the different worlds. Her primary essence, however, had remained in her physical form so that she could keep it alive. Only on special occasions, when others were

105

protecting her body, had she lifted the life spark into the higher planes. Now, her primary essence was free of all physical limitation and she would be able to move throughout the different planes with a greater sense of awareness and intimacy.

She would return alone. Alone, she would continue her destiny. Alone, yet in shared consciousness with her Divine Complement and at one with the knowledge and memory of her own true completeness.

Home in the Fourth Dimension

BOOK ONE

I REMEMBER FAERIE

I remember Faerie.
I remember that
the green is greener and
sparkles in the ever present daylight.

Beyond the world of time
the sun can stay for hours or years
because time is
a product of our minds.

In Faerie,
Nature is our Mother.
We protect and care for Her like
humans care for their infants.

We are proud when she gives
birth to a flower and
we mourn its passage into seed.

Then,
we alight our hearts to see
the seed take hold and again
become a flower.

Beauty is our essence
and love is impersonal.
In Faerie, we do not love
as humans do.
Humans love in a holding way.

Many of us have chosen to
love humans because they can

return love with a dedication
we can only feel for Nature.

However, whereas we are as constant
as the cycles of the Moon,
humans can love dearly once
and then --
they don't.

In Faerie, we are one with each other
and with our Maker.
We realize we may "look" different,
just as different fingers appear
individual -- yet

we know that we are all attached
to a divine hand
which directs our every movement.

We never question this hand,
nor could we imagine
moving without it.

Our thoughts are colors,
and our emotions are melodies.
We dance through life and warmly anticipate
our next step up the ladder of evolution.

The further up we move,
the more consciously we interact with man.
But they seldom know us.

In olden days, shortly after Atlantis,
we interacted and played
with humankind.

But now the veil is heavy indeed,
and our lives are not interwoven.
After Atlantis, there was a Borderland
where we had a strange mixture of
Faerie and Earth.
Members of our evolution
and of the human evolution
interbred and intermingled.

However, as the human kingdom
fell deeper and deeper into the physical,
our two worlds separated
and Borderland became -- no more.

Only in certain areas in
England, Scotland, Ireland, and Wales
is there even a memory
of Borderland.

In these special areas,
if one is attuned,
the ethereal memory of the Earth
can transport a willing, open mind
into an intense experience of the past.

Through reliving the past on Faerie,
humans can begin to release
their illusion of time.

We await you here in Faerie.
Remember us.

Remember yourselves.
You were with us when
you lived in Borderland

and experienced the
oneness of our Soul.

Your wings await you now.
Come

TRY THEM ON!

CHAPTER FOUR

The Return

As Shature returned her vibration to the troubled ethers around Earth, she found that there was much to do. To her surprise, the other three of her group was also there. The spiritual net which had been formed had stopped the Earth from going off its axis and spinning to its disaster, but the poles had changed and the axis had tilted. There was widespread destruction upon the Earth. Mankind was nearly wiped out, but nature had replenished itself.   Mother Earth was resilient and could replace the old and dead parts of Her with new parts of unsurpassed beauty and wonder. Even among the turmoil and suffering of this plane, Shature could see the planet from a new perspective. She could see it as a whole and therefore realize that it was alive. This Earth, that she had hated because it wasn't her beloved Venus, was a creature of life. It was not just a mass of rocks and water, but rather, a living entity. She had been a small speck upon its surface like a flea upon a goat. This entity, this Earth, had seen that it was time to shake free of that which was destructive to her survival.

Shature then acquired a new respect and love for the entity called Earth. She also saw how her negativity had contributed to the condition that she had come to correct. As she moved down into these lower planes to free and assist others, she realized that she must first free and assist herself. She had to face all the negativity which she had contributed to the troubled world and free it from Earth's ethers before she could be of assistance to anyone else. From this perspective, she realized how small and unimportant her problems had been within the grand scale of evolution. What was born would grow to maturity and would eventually fall to its death. The evolutionary cycle that had its peak in Atlantis had come to a close.

Many had learned their appropriate lessons and had been able to move to a higher plane of existence. Unfortunately, many had also lost much of their evolutionary growth and fallen into destruction. As is so at the end of every great civilization, the darkness and light had become extremely polarized. The light had grown to a peak of excellence that allowed the creation of the bridge to a higher consciousness, but the darkness had many eons to grow in its force as well. As always, the evil had wasted its home in its own greed and hunger for power. In between these two poles, were many confused and frightened souls who did not even know that they were dead.

Shature moved among the newly dead trying to get their attention, but her vibration was still above their perception. Would she have to lower her consciousness even more in order to assist them? She was glad she had left her other half in the higher planes so that she would not again become entrapped in these lower worlds. She held his "feel" and vision within her like a lifeline.

"I am here, my One. Just as you are there and can experience me, I can be here and can experience you. Remember that whatever you face, you are not alone. I am with you always."

With these loving words echoing in her mind, she lowered her vibration more and more in order to be visible to the lost ones.

"Shature," she heard a voice, "You must save us. Disaster will soon strike."

"It has struck! Remember, you are dead!" she told them.

"How can you lie to us so? We are awake and together. How can we be dead?"

Most of them turned from her in anger when she told them the truth, but a few were beginning to remember. She could not help the ones who would not face the truth, but gradually a small group gathered about her who were able to face their current status. They were all frightened and angry.

"How could this have happened? Why did our leaders not warn us or try to divert this disaster?"

"They would not listen, just as they will not listen now. Their denial will hold them in this awful place. But your acceptance of the truth will allow you to raise to a higher vibration where you can learn the lessons of your past life and move on."

The bridge of light was still in place except that it was deteriorating quickly from the lowest vibration up. The doubt, fear and anger around the aura of Earth were gradually destroying it. Those who would move up must do so soon or they would lose this cosmic moment and would have to find their own way up alone. Shature was glad that she had her Divine Complement to serve as a beacon for her so that she could return when her work was done.

At last she was convinced that all those who would listen to her had found their way to the bridge. She joined the others who had volunteered to help the newly dead, and they raised their vibration above these planes of death and suffering. She wondered how many eons it would take the souls who would not listen to turn towards the truth.

When she returned to Lamire, she was concerned at the worried look upon his face.

"What is wrong?" she asked.

"Your Earth mate and son are in trouble. Their boat did not leave soon enough and the seas are very treacherous. Vicor and Ramor are trying to guide them, but their joint energies are not enough for the frightened passengers of the boat to hear. Your son is very attuned to the higher planes. Perhaps if you joined your vibration with the others, he could hear you."

Again I must return, she thought. How could she not? She had known human love and the joys of being a mother. There was no question in her mind. It was their destiny to start a new colony, and she must assist them. She lowered her frequency rate. Again, using her Complement as a lifeline, she moved quickly through the troubled ethers of the newly dead to the planes just above the physical. From this vibration, she could see the Earth and at the same time she could see Vicor and Ramor. She joined them in calling her son. There was a high peaked landmass very near, but the boat could easily miss it in the stormy seas. A tidal wave would hit them soon. The boat had traveled far enough from Atlantis to be safe from the continents submersion, but not far enough to be safe from the ensuing tidal wave that would soon overtake them.

The three beings of the higher planes called Vidann because he was the most receptive. However, no matter how urgent their call, he did not appear to hear them. Then Shature realized that their desperate calls were only adding to his fear, which actually made him less receptive. Therefore, they stopped for a moment and each one summoned all the love they could and focused it towards Vidann.

"Follow love," they called, "FOLLOW LOVE!"

Suddenly, he looked in their direction. There appeared to be a look of recognition upon his face. In unison, the three directed Vidann's attention towards the distant land. He ran to the Captain and pointed in that direction. The three upon the higher planes focused their love towards the sea around the boat. Their loving vibration served to diminish the wave action at the same time that it directed the boat to the land. They willed the wind and water to move the vessel toward the nearest safe shore. As the ship pulled into a small harbor, the three focused their thoughts again to Vidann.

"Leave the ship at once and move to high ground."

The boy looked confused. Why did he not feel safe? He moved away from the others on the ship and focused his mind.

"Mother," Shature heard him say. He felt her! He could hear her call. The three repeated their message again, "Leave the boat at once and seek higher ground!"

He focused his eyes as if he heard and he ran to the Captain again.

"We must leave at once and find high ground!"

At first the Captain would not listen, but he remembered that it was the boy who had found the land.

"You have saved us once, my lad. I will trust your instincts again."

"Hurry, hurry," cried the boy. "We have very little time!"

In a flurry of activity, the Captain loaded the boarding boats. They took only what they could carry in their hands for survival. As the boats reached the shore, the passengers immediately disembarked and followed the boy, who was still listening to the calls of love from the higher planes. Some refused to leave the ship, and some refused to leave the shore just to follow the instincts of a boy, but most of them trusted the lad. Or perhaps, they too could hear the call.

The climb up the hill was difficult and slow, as the ascent was quite steep, but at last they found a large cave at the peak of the hill. Just as the last climber reached the safety of the high cave, they heard a roar that sounded like the eruption of a volcano. Off to the southwest (or whatever direction it was, now that the sun seemed to move in a different trajectory than before), they saw an immense wave. They weren't sure that they were high enough.

"Quick," yelled the Captain. "To the back of the cave. We will build a barricade so that if the water enters we will not be pulled out in the backwash."

"The boy has led us astray," cried some in fear. "We would have been safer on the ship."

"No," yelled the Captain. "We would have been capsized or dashed upon these shores. The very voices that warned us to leave our homeland have led us here and we must listen to them through whoever can hear. Now, do not waste time. We must build the barricade."

They worked as one person raising a wall to partially close off the cave. As they finished the barrier, they could hear the onrushing waters. They huddled themselves together at the very back of the cave and used a rope to bind person to person. The peak of the wave entered the cave but did not have the force to break down their barricade. They clung together and were able to stay in the cave even as the waters rushed back out. They stayed bound together for what seemed like forever before they dared to move towards the front of the cave.

"It is safe," said the boy.

Vidann had been correct. Now everyone was willing to trust him, and one by one, they untied themselves and removed a portion of the barricade to look out. The water line was much higher than before and what once had been a mountain was now a small hill. They could see nothing of the small harbor, their ship, or of those who would not come with them. They were alone now; in a place they did not know, with no means of leaving and only their wits to help them survive.

"We must give thanks," some of them said, and they all joined again into one close unit. This time they joined, not in fear, but in thanksgiving.

The three upon the higher planes could feel the gratitude of those below. Vicor could feel the pull of his new body, his unborn daughter, who was the fruit of his union with his earthly mate. He would stay nearby, as a guide until it was time for his rebirth. Ramor was also being pulled to his new life in Egypt. Shature did not want to again enter a physical form, but she also felt she could not return to the higher planes and leave her family in their present state. She wondered if she could continue to reside at this vibration.

Again, Shature was alone.

She had her family and friends on the third dimension, but they would have to meditate and raise their consciousness in order to perceive her. Shature suspected that only Vidann would be able to accomplish that task. She did not wish to live in the and become what those on Earth would perceive as a ghost. She needed to find a safe place in the Astral Plane where she could still hear her son's call. Her son and Jatain were busy with the task of finding a home and surviving and probably would not need her for awhile. Shature decided to find herself a home as well.

The form that she now wore was neither the androgynous light body of her fifth dimensional life on Venus nor the female third dimensional physical body. Her body was in human form and still female, but it was more ethereal than it had been on Earth. She still identified herself as Shature because she was tied to friends and family of that life. She was also tied to Lamire on the higher planes and could call to him much as Vidann could call to her.

As Shature reflected on her body, she also reflected on her environment. When she had been busy with Ramor and Vicor assisting their family and friends from Atlantis she had hardly noticed where she was. They saw Vidann and the others through a dense mist. As she looked around her now, she saw that same mist all about her. If she focused her attention, she could see Earth, but no matter how much she focused, she could see nothing about her but the mist. The light of this plane was constant and without any evident source. She could not measure time because there was no sun or moon to rise or set, and she could not measure distance, as there weren't any landmarks or stars. She wondered how she would proceed in finding a home here.

Shature had learned from her training in Atlantis that in order to travel in the Astral Plane she needed to have an intention of a destination or goal. She thought about where she would like to be. She wanted a place that was safe and peaceful with people around her who were not limited by the third dimension and who were able to understand who she was and where she came from. Shature closed her eyes and focused on her desire. She had learned that her thoughts would initiate the intention and her feelings would give it power. She wanted her new home to be filled with love, so she sent out her intention with the feeling of love. When she opened her eyes, she could sense the physical world, but she could not see it. In the distances she saw what appeared to be a grove of trees. She desired the experience of the trees and felt herself moving toward them in a floating fashion.

As she approached the grove, she could see a group of small beings who where lovingly caressing the trees. They were about the size of her hand and had small round faces with pointed features and sharp, clear eyes. But, when they touched the tree, their third eye shown so brightly that all she could see of their faces was a beautiful, multicolored radiation of light. Their body was like a gossamer gown that fluttered as they flew among the trees. There was just a hint of arms, and their hands could not be seen through the beautiful light that radiated from them. Their legs were more like one leg that looked like a root on the beings near the ground and like a tail feather on the ones higher up the tree. As she looked more closely, she could see that they had the ability to change shape. At one moment they looked like a leaf or a branch and in the next moment they returned to their gossamer gown.

"Are you physical?" she asked as she caught the attention of the group. With their thoughts instead of their voices, they registered confusion.

"What is physical?" they questioned, speaking with one mind.

Shature realized that she would have to change her approach. This world was definitely not physical. There was still no sun, yet she could clearly see the aura that radiated around every living thing. Including her.

"My name is Shature," she said. "What are you called?"

"Oh," they laughed in unison. "We are called the changers."

The changers seemed to be of a group consciousness and spoke telepathically as a unit.

"What are you doing?" asked Shature, happy to have someone to talk to.

"We are assisting this tree to grow new leaves. Everyone here is known by the task they perform. We assist in the change of the seasons. What are you doing?"

"I am looking for a home," said Shature with more loneliness in her voice than she had intended.

The changers circled her and began to touch her much like they had touched the trees. She felt their touches like little starbursts of love and light. What wonderful creatures they were! As they continued to work on her, the old feelings of fear and anger that Shature had felt on Atlantis began to rise to the surface, but only for a moment. The changers seemed to pull these feelings out of her like a poultice. She could see her aura grow brighter and brighter until it encompassed all the changers. Memories of Venus, Lamire, Vidann and her other loved ones on Atlantis filled her heart.

"You feel better now," exclaimed the changers breaking her reverie.

Shature opened her eyes that she had not realized she had closed.

"Yes, I do. Thank you very much."

The changers moved away from her and formed a small huddle, as if they were having a conference. They then broke formation and hovered just before her face in a floating, bobbing motion. These must be members of the fairy folk, thought Shature.

"Yes, we are," they said responding to her thoughts. "You are now in the Land of Faerie. If you wish to follow us, we can take you to our Queen. She will know how to help you."

"Please do. This is a wonderful place. I think that I could be happy here."

"Then follow us."

They formed a V shape like a flock of birds and led Shature through the grove of trees and deeper into the woods. Shature followed them in a running movement that was so effortless, it seemed almost as though she was flying as well. She could feel the radiation of each tree that she passed, and the birds inhabiting them seemed as conscious of her as she was of them. When she asked them about this, the changers looked again in confusion.

"The winged ones assist us. They are our friends. And in return, we assist them," was their reply.

What a wonderful place, thought Shature. All life seemed to work in cooperation with each other and everywhere she saw great beauty. As her small group traveled through the woods, she saw more changers who sent out melodious beeping sounds in salutation. Her group returned the greetings. From this place she could still contact and help her loved ones, but she was not bound by their physical limitations. Shature wondered if she could contact her Complement and felt his reassuring emanations in response. Yes, this is a place in which she could remain, at least for now.

At last, they came upon a clearing in the forest. There were small huts arranged in a circular fashion, and many adults and a few children were going about their chores, or talking and playing. The environment was filled with joy and peace. As she moved into the clearing, the inhabitants of this small village stopped and stared at her. They registered no fear or malice, but only curiosity. They followed her at a distance as the entire group moved toward the largest hut in the village. One of the changers disappeared into the hut. An attractive young woman emerged from it and beckoned Shature to enter.

Upon entering the hut, Shature was surprised to see how spacious it appeared on the inside. In the center of the hut was a small fire and on the other side of the fire sat another woman, who seemed familiar, in a large wooden chair. The changer was perched on her shoulder. Although small in stature, like all the other women in the village, she held herself in such a regal fashion that Shature was sure she was their leader.

"Sit," spoke a voice as clear as a ringing bell as she invited Shature to sit in a similar chair on the other side of the fire.

"I am Tamara. Welcome to my humble home. I hear the changers found you among the trees. You are human, are you not?"

"Yes, I was human, but I'm not exactly sure what I am now."

"You are still within the human evolution, my dear. We occasionally have humans in their physical shells visit us. If they are receptive, they can see us. However, you are presently without that earthly body. For what reason have you come here?"

"I did not wish to return to my physical form, but I also could not bear to leave my loved ones whom I feel need me at this time."

"Would that be the group that just came ashore?"

"How do you know of them?" Shature questioned.

"My dear, space doesn't limit our vision here. Nor does time. In fact, I was somewhat expecting you. We have 'seers' here, like Lynette," said Tamara as she pointed to the one who invited Shature into her home. "We are aware of the troubles on Atlantis and watched as your group and others formed a bridge of light to stabilize the planet and assist those who could accept it to a higher realm. We owe you all a great debt. In saving the planet, you have saved us as well. You may not have been aware of it, but you inspired us to join you in your meditations and in the creation of the bridge. I feel as though I know you even though we have just met today."

"I too felt the familiarity when I first saw you. Are you the Queen of Faerie?"

"Yes, I am, and I sense that you would like to stay here with us. You are, of course, welcome. If you would like, Lynette will assist in finding you a home. We can talk more after you are settled. I believe you will be with us for a while."

"I would like that very much!"

Tamara rose and seemed to look into Shature's soul. Shature felt an engulfing sense of love and acceptance.

"Welcome to Faerie. It is your home for as long as you wish."

Shature stood as well and thanked Tamara for her welcome.

With joy in her heart, Shature followed Lynette to her new home. She could feel Lamire from the higher worlds and wished that she could communicate with him. To her surprise, she heard his voice as if he were next to her.

"We are whole, my One. We are complete. You are at the hand of the long arm of God Goddess, and I live within its heart. Just as I can look upon you, you can look upon me. No time or space shall separate us as we reside together in Spirit!"

Shature was calm and serene as she followed Lynette. Her Complement's words reassured her. She knew that she had made the right decision. Soon they arrived at the place that would be Shature's residence. It was in a small circle of huts that were made of what appeared to be large leaves in the shape of a dome. Upon entering the dome, she found that it was transparent on the inside and opaque on the outside. She felt instantly at home. She thought that she would like a vase of flowers, and then, at her request a lovely vase of her favorite flowers from Venus appeared upon a crystal table. As she thought of candles, a violet one appeared next to the flowers. Her altar was complete. She then thought of a low, soft chair and found one just behind her.

As soon as she filled her thoughts with a desire, it became manifest. Yes, she would like it here. If there were dark forces on this plane, she could feel that she was in a protected location. She could contact her Divine Complement with ease and was awaiting her next adventure. She was happy and peaceful.

The woods around her hut were filled with life. There were creatures that she remembered from Atlantis and others that looked more like they should be on Venus. As she looked at her form, she saw that it was much like it was in her Earth life. Her hands were intricately formed and she could see a small vortex on each of her fingertips and a large one in the palm of each hand. The one on the right hand spun clockwise, and the vortex on the left hand spun counter-clockwise.

When she moved her hands in front of her, she saw that they left a trail of fine glistening dust, and as she moved them up and down, her body began to rise above the ground. She decided that she would go outside to explore and was drawn into the surrounding forest. She moved among the trees in a floating motion that she was quickly becoming accustomed to. As she floated, she moved her hands again and soon rose higher and higher above the ground. To her surprise, she discovered she could fly. She flew around the trees and up to the top of the forest canopy. She remembered that before she met the changers, she was actually flying, but she was so intent on her mission to find a home that she didn't realize what she was doing. Also, then she felt as though she were without a body, whereas now she felt as though she had claimed this form as hers.

It was so wonderful to fly. All the creatures of Faerie could communicate with her and welcomed her to their home. However, then she wondered how her son and Jatain were doing and began to worry. Instantly, she found herself falling. She became afraid and then she fell faster and faster. She could see the ground rising up to meet her. The fear caught in her throat and she started to scream. Then suddenly, she heard a voice from deep within.

"Remember Love, my one!" It was Lamire.

Just before she was about to crash to the ground, she remembered LOVE. The feeling of Love caught her like a net and set her gently onto the cool forest floor. The birds and other creatures ran to her to reassure her that she was fine.

"Yes," she thought. "I must remember LOVE!"

CHAPTER FIVE

Life in Faerie

Shature felt good about her new home in Faerie because it was safe from the fears of Atlantis, and everyone there was so accepting and loving. She could stay there for a long time. However, time in Faerie was different than it had been in Atlantis and very different that it had been in Venus. In her life on Venus, she had lived in the fifth dimension, whereas Faerie was in the fourth dimension. On Venus there was no concept of time or measurement of space. Everything and everyone was in the here and now. Shature first took an embodiment in time and space in Atlantis. Once there, she quickly learned that everything and everyone was measured.

People measured how long time took, how far a distance was, and, much to her sorrow, the worth of men and women was also measured. Some were "good" and some were "bad". Therefore, there was fear because the bad would try to hurt the good or take something from them. Possession was also a new concept that she learned on Atlantis. On Venus, as in Faerie, she had manifested anything she needed and would gladly give it away, as it was an expression of her. If she desired more, she would merely manifest it. However, in Atlantis, people had forgotten this.

Manifestation was much more difficult in the third dimension, and many had been drawn into the practice of Black Magic to fulfill their selfish desires. The members of the Black Robe did not have to earn their own power. Instead, they would find ways to enslave others in order to steal their power from them. The dark forces in Atlantis were the reason Shature had decided to stay in Faerie. She could have taken on another body like many of the others from Atlantis had done, but she chose to stay in Faerie. She was very happy there. She could fly, manifest instantly, talk with Lamire and help Jatain and Vidann back on Earth.

But, still, there was an unfulfilled longing. A longing for more: more freedom, more creativity, more love, and more unity. She learned to suppress these longings and hide them deep within her heart. However, the hidden feelings created a hard spot in her heart. A place that did not believe it could be loved, and therefore it could not.

Shature threw herself into her work, much as she had done in Atlantis. The changers taught her how to assist them and Tamara took her under her wing. Before too long Shature realized that she was now having trouble communicating with her Complement. Shature had heard his voice when she first arrived in Faerie, but after her heart began to close, she found it difficult to communicate with him. Tamara could feel Shature's struggle and one day took her to a special place that only she and the changers knew about. Through the forest behind Tamara's hut was a cliff that overlooked a deep valley. Tamara led Shature to a large rock with a flat top that perched on the edge of the cliff and instructed her to be seated. The valley below had very little growth and its brown dirt stuck out from the surrounding green trees. As Shature sat upon the rock, she began to feel a strong magnetic pull emanating from the valley. She had to resist the urge to jump off the rock and over the cliff. As she stared into the valley, the world around her grew dimmer and dimmer. It was the sound of Tamara's voice that pulled her back.

"My dear, there is a strong vortex here which can allow you to communicate with your higher self. However, this vortex goes in both directions. Therefore, you must be pure of heart before you enter it or you may be swept into the Lower Astral Plane where the tortured or unconscious, newly dead reside. If you open the vortex with love in your heart, you will move into the higher planes. However, if you open the vortex with fear, you will be pulled into the lower Astral. So you must release your past in Atlantis, heal that hardened place in your heart, and create a life for yourself here. I have helped you all I can. It is now time for you to help yourself."

Tamara left Shature alone, sitting on the edge of her strongest desire and greatest destruction. Shature knew that she was being tested to see if she was ready for the responsibility of greater knowledge. She sat there for a very long time.

"When do all the tests stop? When can I return to my Home where none of these challenges exist?" she thought.

Little did she know just how long she would have to wait or how many experiences she would have. At the edge of her mind she remembered that those who had decided to come to Earth from Venus were committed for the duration of the Great Cycle. Shature had forgotten that information as a protection, just as she had forgotten her longings. If only she could communicate with Lamire again, she would be content.

Shature sat in the same spot at the edge of the vortex for what seemed like a very long time. She knew that she had not yet released her life on Atlantis because she could feel the pain of it like a black cloud. Therefore, it would be dangerous to enter the vortex. She wanted to forgive Atlantis, the forces of darkness there and herself, but she did not know how. Why was it so difficult for her to heal and release the past? Had one short incarnation on Earth so disrupted her Venusian nature that she had become a cold and unloving Soul?

As she stared into the valley below, resisting the pull of the vortex, she thought of Home and how she missed it. Gradually, she came to realize that she could not forgive Atlantis because it had taken her away from Venus. Visions of her life there began to rush to her memory so quickly that they blended into each other. Each memory brought more and more love into her consciousness. She cried and laughed and even sang. She sang a song of Love. It was a song that she had sung with Lamire when they were joined as Lamerius in their fifth dimensional form. As she sang, she felt the power of the vortex pull at her stronger than ever. She was not afraid. She was filled with love.

"Lamerius!" she heard the voice of Founteen, her best friend in Venus. "You are here. We have been calling to you on Earth whenever possible, but you have forgotten that you could bi-locate and be in two places at the same time. While in the higher fourth dimensions of Earth known as Faerie, you can also visit us here."

Shature looked at herself and her surroundings. Yes, she was her complete self. She was Lamerius and she was on Venus. Founteen rushed forward and they merged in greeting. Shature was almost overcome with the total unity that a Venusian merging gave, but the greater part of her that was now Lamerius was totally comfortable and completely calm.

"I had forgotten about merging, the complete unity of two into one and then one back into two," explained Shature, or was she Lamerius?

"I don't think that I am even merged within myself. I feel like Lamerius, but I also feel like Shature, who somehow feels separate inside of me."

Founteen smiled warmly, her entire aura turned pink and gold.

"Yes, you must keep that image of Shature alive and somewhat separate, for it is actually the you that awaits your return in the land of Faerie in the fourth dimension of Earth reality. Take the feeling of Shature with you like a friend. I will help you to remember her. If you forget, you will instantly be transported back to Earth. Without your conscious essence, that form of Shature will 'die' and is not your time yet to return to Venus."

Shature did not want to be pulled back to Faerie yet. She would think of herself as Shature. In that way, it would be easier to remember her life on Earth. Interestingly, when she was on Earth she had to continue to remember her life on Venus. And now, on Venus, she had to continually remember her life on Earth. She began to wonder about Shature's body. Was it protected there by the vortex? She had not planned this journey. The world around her began to fade.

"Wait," she heard Founteen's voice in the distance. "Don't return yet. We have something important to show you. It will help you to forgive your Atlantian life."

"How did you know about that?" Shature was instantly back on Venus.

Founteen smiled again. Shature had also forgotten the beauty and feel of a Venusian smile. No wonder she had been so lonely for Home.

"We are able to monitor our volunteers on Earth," answered Founteen. "Especially when they are in the higher dimensions. Your position in Faerie is perfect because it is in one of the middle planes of the fourth dimension around Earth. Just as you are able to monitor your loved ones on third dimensional Earth from there, we are able to monitor you from fifth dimensional Venus. Remember how difficult it was to communicate with Venus while you were on Earth."

Shature nodded.

"Well, it was as difficult for us to communicate with you. The negative thoughts and emotions on Earth and in the Lower Astral Plane are like a psychic storm that blurs the contact in both directions. That is why you were not able to bi-locate from there."

"When I am on Faerie," Shature added, "I can act like a relay system so that you can monitor those on Earth through me."

"That is correct. But come with me now. I don't know how long you will be able to maintain your self in two separate areas. This is your first bi-location here I believe."

Shature nodded.

"Then follow me now, Shature. I will use that name to assist you in remembering that reality and my presence and voice will assist you in remembering the part of you that is Lamerius. They are both real, but you are only visiting your reality as Lamerius and bound to your life as Shature."

"Bound?"

"Yes, your Soul destiny is there."

The term "Soul destiny" brought to Shature awareness that she was again one with Lamire. She felt him within her and her within him. She was androgynous and complete. She was excited about her experience, but she also felt the conflicting emotions of happiness and sorrow.

"Be careful." Founteen's voice was calm yet firm. "If you become emotional it will lower your consciousness and you will be pulled away from us. Excitement comes from and leads to fear. Calm yourself. Yes, you are complete. Here, on fifth dimensional Venus, it is a normal condition. Remember that this androgynous being is who you truly are. No one and nothing can ever take this reality from you!"

Shature calmed herself. She realized that she would have to balance the consciousness of Lamerius and Shature in order to continue her visit on Venus. She closed her eyes and felt the floating sensation of life on Venus, as well as the hard feeling of the rock beneath Shature in Faerie. She realized that the vortex had allowed her bi-location and she used it as an energy field to unite these two portions of herself. In her mind, she felt herself as

Lamerius, holding Shature's hand while she sat on the rock at the edge of the vortex.

"Good" replied Founteen. "You are improving your multidimensional consciousness. It does take some practice. Come, there is someone I wish you to see."

Shature-Lamerius floated alongside Founteen. The movement on Venus was not one of walking as on Earth, and was even lighter than the floating motion on Faerie.

Founteen talked as they moved, "We could instantly manifest ourselves at our location, but I thought you might enjoy another long vision of your homeland."

Yes, Shature was enjoying the vision. So much so that she forgot to respond. It took all of her concentration not to allow the emotions of Shature to pull her back to Faerie.

"See Shature, this is our Home," she kept saying inside herself as she showed the Shature consciousness everything as if she were a small child.

"Look, there are the floating gardens. See how the beautiful flowers are of colors that are not seen on Earth. Listen-- do you hear how they emit beautiful tones and an aroma beyond Earthly imagination? Do you see their roots floating down towards the planet's surface and their faces looking up towards the rays of the Sun?"

Shature went over to the edge of the garden and sang along with the flowers' melody. She reached out and gently stroked the aura of the garden and felt the flowers' presence like a hundred giggly children. She thought of the changers and knew now that they were Venusian also. She realized that her destiny was to assist in the rebuilding and restoration of Faerie. The flowers were telling her all this by vibrating in a way that she could understand them. The damage to the third dimension had been so severe that it had threatened the fourth dimensional Faerie as well. The flowers told her that when she returned to Earth's Faerie, she was to remember their vibration and to whisper it to all the plants there.

"Please take one of us to assist you," they vibrated to her. A small violet flower broke away from its friends and came to Shature. The sacrifice and bravery of that small flower so touched Shature that she almost lost her focus in a flood of Earthly emotions. Just as Venus began to dim around her, she felt the tiny flower tickle her cheek and wipe away a tear.

"Interesting," it vibrated to her. "We don't have those here. What is that falling down your check?"

Shature laughed, "It is a tear. It comes from both joy and sorrow."

"What are 'joy' and 'sorrow'?" vibrated the flower.

"They are emotions. Emotions are something that happens on the third and fourth dimension of Earth. If you come with me, you will have to contend with them."

"What exactly is an emotion?"

"That is a very good question. I have only had one life on Earth, and even less time in Faerie, so I'm not sure that I can answer your question. I only know that they are somewhat like joy, but of a much lower vibration. Some emotions have a feeling that makes you want to merge with them, and some of them have a feeling that makes you want run away. They make you want to go Home to Venus so badly that you feel as though you will fall apart. Do you see how you feel when you have left your flower bed?"

The flower seemed to nod in agreement.

"Well, what if your flower bed was far, far away and you didn't know if you could ever merge with it again? That would create what they call on Earth a 'bad emotion' such as sadness or fear."

"My," vibrated the flower, "I am glad I will have you with me."

"Are you sure you want to go with me? It is much more difficult than you can imagine."

"What is difficult?" vibrated the flower.

"You will see," said Shature as she reached her hand out for the flower to rest on. As it did so, Shature noticed that she had her fifth dimensional, Venusian hands again. They were long, slender, almost translucent and gold in color. When the small flower

141

touched them, there was a moment of merging. Her hand became violet and gold while the flower became gold and violet. She felt the other flowers around her in the safety of their flowerbed. She heard every tone of every flower sing in harmony with each other and with the environment around them. She knew the sensation of color, the pull of the gravity of Venus, and the warm glow of the Sun. She felt the security of the flowerbed around her and the welcome love rays of the passersby as they admired her.

"Now I know what an emotion is!" shuddered the small flower. It had felt her Earthly life just as she had felt its Venusian life. Shature looked again and saw that its bright violet had dimmed almost to gray. She took the small flower into both hands and cradled it by her heart. She then remembered her love for Jatain, her mate in Atlantis. She remembered the birth of her son and the feeling of him suckling her breasts. She remembered the laughter and the camaraderie of Temple life, and she remembered Ramor. She was taken from her reverie by the tickle of the small flower in the center of her cupped hands. She looked at it and saw that it was not only its natural color, but also more vibrant. It seemed to have octaves of radiation that were not present in its aura before. Its tone was now fuller with more complex, even more beautiful harmonies. And, yes, the flower was actually larger. It had grown to almost twice its original size.

"Now I understand 'good' and 'bad' emotions!" it vibrated. "I am ready to go with you. I understand what I must face, but I will use your courage as an example."

"My courage," thought Shature. She had never thought of herself as courageous. She had only done what she had to.

"Oh, but you were very courageous."

"Who was that voice," thought Shature. It was so familiar. She turned gradually so that she would not become too excited and drop her vibration. Yes, she saw from the corner of her eye, that it was whom she thought. It was Ramor!

"Ramor," she went to him and they merged. In the merging, she knew that he too was bi-locating.

"I thought you had taken on another Earth body, how can you come here from the third dimension?"

"Yes, I have taken a body, but it is an infant and I can still leave my body in the care of his mother. Soon I will be too old, but I heard from Founteen that you needed me."

"You could hear Founteen while you had a body?"

"Yes, since my body is still an infant, a large portion of my essence is still in the fourth dimension. When I get a little older, I will need to put most of my essence into my physical form so that I can do my work there. Until then, I can enjoy visiting Home as often as I wish."

"Oh, Ramor, I was brought here because I could not forgive my Atlantian life, but this small flower has taught me how to do so," she said as she held out her hands with the flower softly nestled inside her cupped palms. "I also had many wonderful experiences in Atlantis that I had forgotten. In order to help the flower, I remembered them, which helped me as well. I know now that third dimensional life is filled with the polarities of good and bad so that we can learn about making the right choices in creating the life that we desire."

"And knowing you was always a good experience," said Ramor as he took the flower from Shature's palms and placed it in her hair just above her right eye. The aura of her third eye made the flower larger, brighter, and more harmonic.

"This is my new flower bed. Let's go home!" the flower vibrated.

In a flash, Shature was again in Faerie. She sat upon the hard rock and saw the faint flicker of the vortex before her. She reached up to her hair and, sure enough, there was the flower. It was a piece of Home and a new friend.

When Shature returned to the Faerie Ring, the name used for the cluster of homes formed in a circular pattern, Tamara was the first person that she saw. Tamara looked at Shature's aura and the beautiful violet flower in her hair and said simply, "I see you have been to Venus."

Shature was not surprised by Tamara's remark. Tamara seemed to know everything that happened here. Shature smiled.

"I was complete again! Now I know that I can visit Home if I want to. I was told that my new friend and I," Shature pointed to the flower, "are ready to assist you in healing the fourth dimension."

"Yes," replied Tamara, "with the many who died in such fear during the fall of Atlantis, the Lower Astral Planes are very disturbed. Our world is in danger of lowering its vibration because the pull of the dark energy and the destruction is so great. Your Venusian friend will be greatly needed. The changers will be very happy to meet it. Shall we go find them now?"

Shature nodded in agreement and they took off together to find the changers. However, unknown to them, they were being watched. The Dark Robes in the Lower Astral Planes had banned together in order to increase their power. They could, if they performed their secret rites, view the land of Faerie. They found it much better than the planes of dissonance and darkness to which their Souls had passed. Perhaps, if they watched closely, they would be able to find a way to gain entry. They were very curious about the flower that the newcomer named Shature carried in her hair. If they could obtain it, perhaps it would give them the means to enter Faerie. But how could they get it? They would have to watch and wait.

They could not die now and could wait for all of eternity.

Shature continued to release the pain from her life in Atlantis and was soon able to communicate with Lamire again. Everyday her heart healed more. She named the Venusian flower Violet and together they worked with the changers to heal the land of Faerie. Normally, whatever occurred on Earth did not affect the fourth dimension, but the sinking of Atlantis was such a cataclysm that it even affected portions of the fourth dimension. And, the lowest plane of the fourth dimension, the lower Astral, was still turbulent with the fear of the many who had died in terror.

"This fear pulls at the energy of love which is the binding force of the universe," a changer told Shature while they worked together.

"How does fear pull at love?"

"Well," it replied. "Do you see how we send love to the new children of Nature?"

Shature nodded.

"From where do we send this love?'

"From our hearts and minds combined." Shature had been learning her lessons.

"Good, now think of a frightening thought."

Shature didn't want to remember the many frightening thoughts she had had in Atlantis, but she did so at the request of the changer.

"Now combine your heart and mind and send love."

Shature tried to do so, but her heart would not cooperate. It seemed to be repulsed by the thoughts of the frightened mind and would not merge with it.

"Now," continued the changer because she could see Shature's struggle. "Release those frightened thoughts."

Shature tried to do so, but they churned around in her mind like an evil wind.

"Think of something or someone that you love," said the changer.

Shature thought of flying, but she crashed into a tree. She thought of dancing, but she missed a step. How quickly the negative thoughts burrowed into all areas of her mind, she thought. At last she thought of Venus. She thought of the purple trees that swung their long, hanging branches with the morning breeze. She thought of the yellow sky and the lovely reddish tint of the Sun. She remembered merging with her friends and she remembered being ONE with Lamire.

"There," said the changer. "Now your heart and mind are one and you didn't even try."

"Yes, I was thinking of Venus and Lamire." She smiled.

"Did you see how fear pulled your heart and mind apart? It is the same, of course, if there is a feeling of fear in your heart because then your mind loses its reason and can think only of survival and finding protection."

"How do you know this?" Shature asked the changer. "You have never been to Earth and experienced the fear there."

"Oh, but you are wrong. We were on Earth from the very beginning. On Mu we lived with the humans just as we now live with the fairies. We even lived in Atlantis before its vibration became too low. We are builders of form and we can only resonate to the vibration of love. Once fear lowers a vibration, we must raise it with the love vibration like a leaf in an upwardly rising breeze. We cannot exist in an atmosphere of fear. We simply disappear. Of course, we don't really disappear, but it appears that way to those still in the lower vibration.

"Now we do our work in Faerie, where all nature is loved and appreciated. We can still interact with the humans on Earth if they create a place for us that is filled only with love and appreciation. Then they can call to us with their love and we can temporarily enter that place to boost the natural growth of nature and bless the humans as well.

"Aren't you afraid that the humans will hurt you?" asked Shature from within her own fear.

The changer smiled and its tiny face lit up.

"We only exist in Love!" was its only response.

148

Shature and Violet were so busy with the changers that the vortex was almost forgotten. Violet was a big hit among the changers but remained Shature's constant companion maintaining its position somewhere in her aura. Eventually, the flower and the person became one. Shature had an ever-present reminder of Home, and Violet had the constant experience of Faerie. Atlantis was far behind her now. Shature was comfortable and happy in her new life. She had not heard from her family on Earth for a long time until, one day, she heard a call that came from deep within her Soul. She could not make it out at first, she returned to the large rock by the vortex and listened carefully.

It was her son, Vidann. Time on Earth was very different than it was on Faerie and, though Shature had not appeared to age at all, Vidann was now a grown man. His father Jatain had become old and was now breathing his last breath. Vidann was preparing to become the leader of their band. He had served as his father's Councilor and as Spiritual Leader of their band for many years and his right to become the next leader was undisputed. However, Jatain had lain in the area between life and death for almost two months of Earth time. He appeared to be suffering greatly, but he could not release his body. In desperation, Vidann was calling to Shature again for assistance.

Over the Earth years, Shature had guided them many times from her place in Faerie. She would assist them in choosing safe locations to live and people whom they could and could not trust. After the fall of Atlantis, the land had greatly changed. Once the island had been mountainous, but the great flood had raised the water level. The island was now smaller and appeared almost flat. There were many barely surviving who wandered around in small, primitive groups. Many of them asked to join with Jatain's group because it was well organized and communicated with the spirit world. But only those who could dedicate themselves to honoring Light and the Goddess energy of the planet were allowed to join their band. Jatain had seen the results of selfish disregard for nature and would not associate with those who could not honor the sacredness of Earth.

"Civilization" was very primitive in the area where Jatain and Vidann found themselves. Many Priests of the White Robe had journeyed to other lands when they saw that Atlantis was doomed, but few had come to this land, which would much later be known as Ireland. The energies of Jatain and Vidann's home were very akin to those of Faerie. The natives of this land had revered and respected the "little folk" for all remembered time. As Shature watched over them she was careful to keep her vibrations high so that she could not fall victim to the still troubled plane between Earth and Faerie. She had learned that the members of the Dark Robes had banned together and were probably watching her just as she was watching her family on Earth. She tried to remember the advice of the changers about fear and love, but sometimes she felt the darkness so strongly that fear began to pull upon her. She would then have to cease all communications with Vidann or her fear might attract the attention of the dark forces to him.

Shature wondered if the Dark Robes were somehow responsible for Jatain's entrapment. She went to Tamara for advice, but Tamara told Shature that she could not help. Shature would have to find the answer inside her. What could she do? Would she have to expose herself to the Lower Astral Plane in order to help Jatain? She knew that she could not ponder long, for time moved much more swiftly on the Earth plane and she knew that her dearly loved Jatain was suffering. Also, Vidann had said that their band was becoming more and more disorganized because they were between leaders. Jatain had become gravely ill very suddenly and had not had time to announce his son as the new leader. Shature knew that her only choice was to enter the vortex and go to Jatain. She would leave Violet with the changers and journey down into the vortex alone.

"No" vibrated Violet. "We cannot be apart. We are one now."

"But you are newly from Venus and will not be able to tolerate the density there, even in your ethereal form."

"We must be one so that you can remember to vibrate only to Love."

Shature knew that Violet was right. If she allowed even a moment of fear to enter into her consciousness, the Dark Robes could pull her into their lair. At last she went to Tamara and told her what she must do.

"I will wait by the vortex and anchor your vibration in Faerie," she said. "I will hold vigil and will not leave my meditation until you return."

"Thank you, Tamara. You are a true friend indeed!"

Shature gave her a warm embrace. The changers gathered around Tamara at the edges of the vortex.

"We, too, will assist you and Violet." They spoke as one.

Shature could wait no longer. She allowed the vortex to pull at her consciousness. She held Violet in her hand, pressed to her heart, in order to remember the Love vibration of Home. She fell into the pull of the vortex and in an eye blink she was in a wooden lodge. It was located next to a large river at the edge of a forest. Before her she saw the dying form of Jatain lying in his warrior's robe upon a large animal skin. He had had to become a warrior and eat of the flesh in his journey into the unknown territory. Shature had had all her previous communications with Vidann, so she barely recognized the man who lay before her. He was no longer the young Priest she had known in Atlantis, but his essence was the same, as was the love she held for him. In Atlantis, he had always shaved his face in memory of his Venusian self and worn only finely woven cloth. Now he had a rough white beard and his costume was of deer hide. But his heart was as pure as ever. Except, he wasn't completely there. There was a small portion of his essence, just small enough to keep his body barely alive, but the rest of his soul was gone! But where?

"Mother," she heard Vidann's call. The others in the room could not see her and slunk from the room when they saw Vidann communicating with Spirits again. That is except for one woman who was heavy with child.

"This is Alicia, my mate," spoke Vidann.

"Can she see me?" asked Shature.

"Yes I can, dear Mother. But I believe it is only because of my child. He is to be a seer, like your son."

Shature knew that Jatain had not wanted to die because he wanted to see the birth of his first grandchild. However, in waiting too long at death's door, something had gone wrong. Shature could smell the presence of the Dark Ones trying to invade the room. Deep inside she heard a laugh.

"We will trade the Soul of this man if you give us the flower."

Shature's hand reflexively flew to Violet who had returned to her hair. For just a moment she felt fear, just a glimmer, but it was enough. Her vision of Vidann and his mate began to fade, as did their vision of her.

"Mother," he called, "Remember me! Remember My Love!"

But it was no good. Shature was being pulled into a vortex again, but this one was different. This one was evil. She could barely see Vidann now. He seemed to know what was happening. She could see him battling his own fear, and then a ray of recognition went across his eyes. He ran to an alcove at the other end of the lodge and returned with a statue. It was the Venusian Mother Goddess. He held it high and began to sing - *in Venusian* - a song that his father must have taught him. Shature conquered her fear as she heard the tones of Home. Violet doubled in size and vibrated harmonious tones to the song of Venus. Alicia also joined in the song, as did her unborn child. Shature filled with Light and Love.

"Thank you, dear son," Shature sent her message to him on a beam of love. "You have saved me. Continue your chant. I must retrieve your father."

Vidann smiled and held the statue higher above his head. It was garlanded with fresh flowers and studded with jewels he had found on his journeys. It had been the one thing he had grabbed from the ship and carried up the hill. Shature looked again to the dying form of Jatain, and next to him she saw the journal that she had given him when she had given Vidann the statue as they departed Atlantis without her. They both had remembered to take their one gift from her in their moment of terror. Now, she would remember them. She turned and faced the vortex that she had been resisting.

"Are you ready?" she asked Violet.

In response, the flower vibrated to a deeper hue and its tones emitted more harmonics. Their light preceded them as they entered the vortex. When they finally reached the darkness at the end of the vortex, the Dark Robes had to shield their eyes.

"I come in Love and Forgiveness. I believe you have someone dear to me. My love shall release the bonds of darkness that your magic has used to trap him. But I hold no malice towards you. I understand that you, too, wish the enjoyment of my friend Violet. Although I cannot release the flower to you, I will gladly give you one of its seeds. However, it will not grow into a flower without light and love. If you care for it and tend to it gently, it, too, will become a flower--a flower of my Home. A Home that you also can return to when you remember who you truly are."

Shature reached up to Violet who lovingly surrendered one of its seeds to her. She walked between the rows of now cowering Dark Robes and opened the vessel that held the essence of Jatain. A ray of Light and a warm breeze ruffled through the dense air of the cave of the Dark Robes as Jatain's soul was released. Shature placed the seed inside the vessel, but kept the lid for herself.

"Love grows best in freedom," she stated.

"Now," she turned to address the Dark Robes around her. "Who will tend this seed?"

Many of them turned in horror and rushed from the cave. But, three, or was it four, seemed to lighten their aura and move toward her. She handed one of them the vessel and the others gathered around him. In the recesses of the cave, she heard a yell, the sound of running feet and the clanging of metal.

"Now, Mother – Now!" she heard her son.

She allowed his love to guide her back and the essence of Jatain followed. When she returned to the Lodge, his essence returned to his form. For a moment, Jatain was awake and sat up.

"Shature! You are here to take me Home."

Then he was dead. All of his life force rose into the higher planes and united with his higher self.

"Thank you Mother," Vidann and Alicia spoke together. Shature wrapped her essence around Vidann and felt his love again. Memories of his infancy and boyhood came to her. She felt such joy that she was almost pulled back to Faerie. But first she must embrace Alicia. As she did so, she felt something very familiar. It was---it was---Lamire. The child was to be inhabited by the Soul of Lamire!"

"Tamara, Lamire is going to take on a body," were Shature's first words when she returned through the vortex. Violet was as far from her aura as it had ever been because the changers were so happy to see it again.

"I know," said Tamara.

"You knew? Why didn't you tell me?"

"Because Lamire asked me not to. He had petitioned to be in Faerie with you. The Council of Seven has told him that since you and he are Complements, he must have at least one physical incarnation before he joins you in Faerie"

"Joins me in Faerie!!! Do you mean that we can be one again?"

"No, dear, the vibration is still too low here to be joined in the same form, but you can be mates, like you were with Jatain in Atlantis. And you can help him while he is on Earth, just as you have helped your son, and as Lamire helped you when you were physical."

The joy that filled Shature was almost more than she could bear. She knew how quickly Earth lives passed. Then they could be mates. And think of the work they could do together! Between the two, they could work to help heal the Lower Astral Plane and increase the communication between Faerie and Earth. If the humans of Earth thought like the members of Faerie, they would never bring about a cataclysm such as what happened on Atlantis. She and Lamire could work as one to teach the people of Earth to love the Goddess and to revere all of Her creations.

BOOK ONE

Return to the Third Dimension

BOOK ONE

THE KISS

Dear Love,
so soft and gentle
you kissed my lips today

Silent as
a morning cloud
you came into my dream

You reached for me and
pulled me through
the limits of my mind

Then palm to palm
and heart to heart
the worlds between us blurred

But with your kiss
my world came back
and I was left alone

Oh, but alone
shall never be
what once it was for me

For all my life
the memory of

your kiss upon my lips

shall draw me back
into your world —
the place where we are ONE

In that Oneness
I shall know
the being that I AM

With open heart
I think with love
and love with peaceful mind

Polarities extend beyond
the limits they have known
and you and I shall live inside

THE SILENCE OF OUR LOVE.

CHAPTER SIX

Malton's World

Vidann named his son Shaturn, after his mother. Since Alicia had almost died giving birth, Shaturn was an only child. That was part of the divine plan, because he had a very powerful destiny and needed much love and attention to achieve it. Shaturn took over his father's role as leader even before Vidann's death. His father had not wanted to take the chance that he would be caught between life and death, and the band would again be leaderless. Shaturn lived a long life and had many children. He had six daughters and five sons. He also had three wives, as two of them had died in their rugged lifestyle. When at last Shaturn died, he left a powerful legacy. He had maintained in contact with Shature for most of his life, and together they had established a strong attachment between the ways of Faerie and Earth.

The four who had taken Violet's seed had indeed loved it into a flower. Perhaps they did so in order to possess a flower of their own, but once they had experienced love, they found it more satisfying than greed and fear. The four, along with their flower, did much to heal the Lower Astral Plane. They also created a safe passage between Faerie and Earth through which Shaturn and Shature traveled many times.

The final passage was at Shaturn's death. Shature knew his time was near. He had given his position to his eldest daughter to further continue the way of the Goddess. He was ready to leave Earth. When Shature answered his call, she again found an old man in leathers and a long white beard. He was so surrounded by his large family that the lodge was filled to the walls. When Shaturn's spirit rose from his body, a warm breeze filled the room and there was the scent of flowers and a soft melody. Shature embraced him and together they entered the vortex into Faerie.

Shature and Lamire were together in Faerie for a thousand years. From time to time Lamire would take a body to keep the connection between Faerie and Earth, but Shature refused to take on another physical form. When Lamire was in a physical form, Shature still communicated with him and they worked together much as they did in Faerie. But, at the close of their thousand years together, Lamire took on a body and forgot. He forgot Faerie, he forgot Spirit, and he forgot Shature. Shature watched him grow into a man and tried to contact him again and again. Still, he did not remember.

He was a prince of one of the many small kingdoms in the land that was later to be known as England. His name was Malton. There was much fighting that had to be done in order to secure their small kingdoms. He enjoyed his power, he enjoyed his possessions, and he enjoyed fighting. He liked being a man and he believed, as did his father, that women were weak and inferior. His only spirituality was of the sword and his greatest loves were fighting, drinking and whoring. Shature was very upset. Lamire, now known as Malton, embodied the very consciousness which had destroyed Atlantis and which they had worked so hard in Faerie to heal. He had no love for the land, other than to own it. If a sacred tree were in his way, he would chop it down. He loved to hunt and would often kill more than he could eat just for the sport of it and leave the animal where it had died.

He had been born into this life as the youngest child and the only boy with seven sisters. His father, whom he became exactly like, spoiled him mercilessly. Both Malton and his father had violent tempers and saw nothing wrong with hitting a woman if she "deserved" it. When they took a new territory, they took the women as well. Malton had many bastard children, but would claim none of them as his child. Nor would he marry. At first his father thought his son's behavior admirable, but he was getting old and wanted to see a grandson before his death. He began to nag his son,

"Marry now. You can still play around. Do you think I was loyal to your mother? However, she was always with child," he said again and again over their cups.

Father and son loved to drink together and would often fall asleep on the floor of their great hall. The servants then would remove their boots and cover them with skins. The father would awake like an angry bear

"Bah—who took my boots." He, of course, had forgotten that it was he who instructed his servant to remove them. Malton would laugh and call a servant for morning mead. If the servant were young and pretty, he would take her right in front of everyone on the floor of the great hall. Then his father would laugh uproariously. His many cups of mead had long ago taken away his ability to do the same, much to the relief of his wife. Now, his only sexual pleasure was in watching his son. From her place in Faerie, Shature watched this scene over and over. What could she do? Malton was everything that Lamire had avoided. She must find a way to save him

"You cannot interfere with his free will." Tamara said repeatedly. "He is living the life he has chosen."

"How could he have chosen to be such an ogre? My beloved Lamire is lost to me. I must help him remember who he is."

"It is not good to interfere," warned Tamara. "In fact, it is very dangerous. You can become caught in the very trap which you wish to free him from."

"I have to take that chance."

"Shature, you are being as greedy as he is. You had a thousand years in Faerie together. Do you know how long that is in Earth years?"

But Shature refused to listen. She became obsessed with "saving" Malton. She would have to go there herself!

"Do you mean to take a body?" asked Tamara.

"Oh no! I will go there as myself — a fairy."

"But he doesn't believe. You will have to take on great material density in order for him to see you. Be careful Shature. What you are pondering is very, very dangerous."

Still Shature would not listen.

"Perhaps there are greater powers at work here," thought Tamara aloud.

She decided to stop fighting Shature, and she also stopped listening. Everyone was becoming upset by Shature's constant worry. Finally, Tamara went to Shature.

"If you must go to him, do it now or stay to your own council. You are doing as much damage here as he is there. Have you noticed how dull Violet has become?"

Shature instantly reached for her friend. Indeed it was much smaller and its colors were indeed dim. Its tone was not audible and it even looked limp.

"Oh Violet, what have I done? Tamara is right; I must go down there now. Violet you must stay with the changers."

"But I have never left you," it weakly vibrated.

"I know that you have been my constant companion, but you can't be with me this time. It is too dangerous, and I have weakened you greatly. No wonder the changers have been avoiding me. They could not stand to see you suffer."

Violet was too weak to argue more.

"I will take you to the changers now. When I see that you are well, I will leave."

The changers were difficult for Shature to find because her vibration had become abrasive to them. Finally, she calmed herself enough to raise her consciousness enough to "see" them.

"We were here all along Shature. We did not avoid you. It was just that your vibration had become so dissonant that you could not see us. It is good that you go to Lamire now. If you don't, soon you will find yourself in the Lower Astral Plane."

Shature shuttered. As much as she had avoided Earth, she found it far preferable to the Lower Astral Plane. Perhaps there *was* a higher power at work. She had avoided the Earth plane so much that she was beginning to fear it. She had to face that fear. As soon as Violet recovered, she would go to Malton. Perhaps an encounter with a fairy woman would help him remember.

If only she could find a way to make him see her.

While Shature waited for Violet to recover, she monitored Malton from her home in Faerie. At last, she saw her opportunity. Malton had developed a high fever from a sword wound and was hallucinating. Perhaps he could be receptive to her in that altered state. Violet was doing fine now. Shature left it in the care of the changers and returned to the vortex. She entered the vortex to lower her vibration as she had done when she communicated with Lamire in his other Earth lives. Luckily, along with the four guardians of Violet's seed, a relatively safe passage was created through the lower astral.

"Malton, Malton," she sang his name as she hovered above his prone body. His glazed eyes looked in her direction. He slapped away the servant who was attending him and rose on his elbow. Even in his illness, he was a beautiful man. His wild yellow hair and short beard were wet from sweat, but his arms were still massive and his chest was like a bear. His eyes were of a penetrating blue with just a glimmer of recognition as he looked in her direction. She appeared to him as a pink gossamer presence.

"Go away!" he yelled. "I'm not ready to die."

"You will not die," she sung to him in her Faerie voice. "It is merely a fever. Take some rugroot and it will heal you."

Malton had avoided all the "witch" healer women, but the vision before him almost frightened the brave warrior. He knew he could not own nor kill this vision, so he decided he must listen to it.

"Get me one of those witch healers," he tried to yell, but was too weak.

"Yes, my lord," answered the servant in disbelief.

When the healer arrived, Malton said, "Rugroot, I must have rugroot!" Then he passed out.

The healer had heard of rugroot, and knew where it grew, but had never used it for fevers. However, she knew not to disobey Prince Malton.

"Yes, my lord," she responded to the now unconscious Prince.

Much to the healer's relief, the rugroot worked.

"Please, my lord," she asked on her final attendance of him. "How did you know about the rugroot?"

"What are you talking about?" he growled.

As his strength returned, his vision receded from his memory. The healer's words jarred his memory. He recalled the beautiful woman in the gossamer pink -- pink as the wild roses of his homeland. Bah — he had no use for flowers. Had he grown soft in his illness? But the vision had been planted. Shature would wait.

Shature came to him in his sleep, as it was the only time that he was receptive. Night after night, Malton had dreams of a beautiful woman in gossamer pink. What was wrong with him? The only use he had for women was for his own pleasure. He had never cared for them. This one was not even real. However, he could not banish the vision. He became obsessed. In all his life, he had never experienced something, or someone that he could not own. Perhaps he was enchanted! "This has to be a Faerie woman," thought Malton. With this realization, he began to see her in his waking life as well. Just in the corner of his eye as he was hunting or riding through the forest. He began to look for her rather than for deer, and he began to ride slowly through the woods, rather than running his horse. For the first time in his life, he began to "see" the world around him. Before he only noticed what he wanted to take for himself. The rest was irrelevant. Then, gradually, in looking for the beautiful woman, he began to see the beauty around him. He lost his taste for mead and fighting in the great hall, and even for whoring with the servants. The Faerie woman was the only one he wanted. He must have her.

His father became worried and blamed his illness and the healer as well. She had to flee in the night to find safety in another village. Shature had warned her and had led her through the thick woods to the next village. The healer believed in Faerie and instantly recognized Shature.

"You must flee. The King blames you for the change in his son. Quickly, I will lead you to safety."

The healer was young and had no family. She believed the Faerie woman and followed her without question. She, too, had noticed the change in the young Prince. In fact, everyone did. Now the King was becoming embarrassed. He called his son to him.

"Malton, something is wrong with you since your illness. Go into the woods alone and find what you seek. You are upsetting my entire kingdom. I want my son back. I miss him."

"Yes, Father, you are right. I must find what is plaguing me."

"But beware of the western woods. Many call them the Enchanted Forest and say they are the gateway to the Faerie Kingdom. Those who enter there, do not return," were his father's parting words.

Malton left at dawn the next morning. The King was worried to send his son out alone, but he was more worried about what would happen to Malton if he stayed. Once he was out in the woods, he would find himself again. Perhaps he would even find this woman and bring home a wife. Then the King would have a grandson at last. Malton headed straight for the Enchanted Forest. He had searched the entire kingdom for this maiden. She must be a Faerie or else he would have found her. He was not afraid, he told himself. He had never been afraid of anything or anyone. He would find this Faerie woman and bring her to his castle. He must!

Shature was well aware of Malton's thoughts. Tamara was right. She had started something dangerous, even unnatural. Nothing good could come from this, but now she had to see it through. She had lowered her vibration so much in order to make herself visible to Malton, that it was becoming difficult to find and enter the vortex back to Faerie. Luckily, the four who had taken Violet's seed had offered her refuge in their cave. Just as Malton had lost a large portion of his nature, she had lost a large portion of hers. The Enchanted Forest was the perfect place for them to meet.

173

She didn't need to lower her vibration further and since Malton entered the woods expecting to see a Faerie, his consciousness was attuned to that higher vibration.

Shature began to follow him as he moved slowly through the woods. He had his sword drawn and was very tense. She would wait to show herself when he felt more comfortable. Shature knew that much of Maltons's attraction to her was that she was the first thing in his life that he could not instantly take. She had to be careful. If he found her too easily, he would lose interest. She feared that once he conquered her, she would be forgotten. She was wise to have that fear. Life long habits can change in a moment of crisis, but tend to return once life is as it always was. Shature had no interest in the life of Malton's mother. She would awaken Malton to his higher self, and then she would return to Faerie — somehow!

Malton wandered through the Enchanted Forest for almost a moon cycle. Each day he would feel her closer, and each evening he would dream of her. He dreamt over and over that the faerie woman and he were mates in another land and time. It was a place unlike any place he had known. Of course, he had only known his own kingdom. But this place was different. There was a small flying person around the woman and she always wore a beautiful violet flower in her hair. And the flower was almost human. It could talk to them, and it changed colors and size according to its mood.

"This is ridiculous," he thought. "Dreams have many unreal components."

He had never remembered his dreams before his sword injury. Every evening he fell asleep from the heaviness of mead. Or he was in the field as a warrior or a hunter. However, he'd had neither mead, nor women, nor battle since his illness. He hardly recognized himself. He *had* become soft, and he was definitely enchanted. There had been only a glimpse of pink out of the corner of his eye, but no sign of this mysterious woman. He must stop this ridiculous behavior. He had become the laughing stock of the entire kingdom. His father was right. He would go home and return to his duties and his old life. He hungered for the taste of mead, for the pretty wench that served it, and the fight that would follow.

"Were you looking for me?"

Shature knew that it was time to appear because he was returning to his old self. Malton turned to the tone of the beautiful, melodious voice. It was she--the woman of his vision. And now he could see her clearly. Her hair was long and as golden as his was. Her face looked familiar, even though he had never been able to see it in his visions. Her eyes appeared to be a violet color and were unusually large and tilted upwards at the temples. Her nose was small and her chin was pointed. And yes, so were her ears. Her ears were pointed as well! What was this creature? She could not be human!

"I am from the kingdom of Faerie," she responded to his unspoken words. "I am your Complement and I have come here to help you remember who you are."

"Bah"—his old self returned with his mounting fear. "I know who I am. I just don't know who you are. Why have you been enchanting me?"

"I just told you," she replied in a lilting voice.

As she spoke, her body floated up and down. It was then that he realized that her feet did not touch the forest floor. He impulsively reached for his sword.

"That will do you no good here. You are in the Enchanted Forest, and I am of a higher vibration than you are at this moment. Your sword would go right through me. Try it." She dared him.

"I would not strike an unarmed woman," he said with dignity.

"That is not what I have observed."

"What? Have you been spying on me?"

"I guess you could say I was, but actually I have been spying on us. You and I are One."

"You speak nonsense." He roared. "I am imagining you. I have been touched since the illness and I have been in these infernal woods for far too long. Something is wrong here. I have not been able to kill a single deer and I am a master huntsman." He boasted.

"Yes, the deer here are protected. But several smaller members of the animal kingdom have sacrificed themselves so that you could eat. And, the 'small ones' have shown you roots and edible berries. You are well. I can see it in your aura."

"My aura, small ones, animals sacrificing themselves for me? I must be ill again. It is time to leave these woods. My father was right. No woman is worth this misery!"

"Even your Divine Complement?" she chimed. "I am Shature, beloved, don't you remember me?"

He looked at her again and saw a violet flower in her hair and saw that the sky around her was yellow. He felt a moment of love. Love, that was an emotion with which he was unfamiliar. His father had whisked him away from his mother as soon as he was suckled. He knew pride, possession and dedication. But he had never known love. And then, just as quickly, the vision was gone.

He rubbed his eyes to clear his vision, but she was still there. However, the flower was gone and the woods were green again.

"Where is your flower?" He asked before he had a chance to stop himself.

"You remembered!" she started to rush to him in joy, but backed away when he recoiled from her in horror.

He had hardly heard his own question, his old self was returning. "If you knew I was in here starving for a moon cycle, why did you come to me only now?"

"You were not starving. You eat too much meat and drink too much mead. It lowers your vibration."

"Lowers my vibration? You are talking nonsense again. Answer my question," he demanded.

"I am not one of your servant women. You cannot command me."

Then, she disappeared before his eyes.

"Now I've done it," he said under his breath. "How will I get her back?"

"You must apologize," he heard her whisper in the air. He looked around, but she was still gone.

"Apologize! I am Prince Malton. I apologize to NO ONE."

There was no reply. The woods around him were dead still and totally quiet. There were no bird sounds, no insects, and even the breeze had stopped.

"Good," he said to himself. "She is gone. Now I can go home."

But where was home? He could not find the Sun through the density of the trees; he could not find direction from the breeze, which had ceased. It was only then that he realized that he had been wandering for an unknown time, as if he were in a trance. He had not kept track of where he was going or where he had been. His horse, his one companion, suddenly became frightened. He, too, could feel that something was wrong. It was as if the woods were angry. It was as if she were the spirit of the woods. He led his horse, calming him as they walked through the woods. But where were they walking? He tried to follow his own tracks, but they were gone as if by magic. Yes, this was the feeling around him. It was magic.

"You are using your magic to try to frighten me!" he yelled into the woods.

There was no reply, but he heard in his head.

"I don't use magic, I am magic!"

He shook his head. This was a dream and soon he would wake up.

179

But he didn't wake up. He continued to wander through the woods. But it was no use. He left trail markers for himself, but when he tried to retrace them, they were gone. Then he began to see things--things that had only caught the corner of his eye before, were now entering his full vision. He saw a streak of light, and then it became a small creature with wings. Then it was gone. It was, however, the only clue he had so he decided to follow it.

Soon there was not one streak of light, but many, and the birds came back, hundreds and hundreds of them. Each of their individual songs blended into a concert of birdsong as they all followed the streaks of light. Malton knew instinctively that he was being led deeper and deeper into the Enchanted Forest, but he had lost his fear. The mystery was revealing itself to him. This vision he had had was a Faerie woman, and he was entering the Faerie Kingdom. His mother and sisters had told him about Faerie when he was a small boy until his father forbade them to ever speak of it again.

Suddenly, he was homesick for his mother and sisters. He hadn't thought of them in years. When he was a small boy, he would sneak away from his father to visit them, and always his father would follow him.

"Stay away from women," he said. "Bed them if you must, but don't listen to them."

His father's words had hurt him deeply when he was a child. He loved his mother, and she loved him. Love, yes, there had been love in his life. His mother and sisters had adored him, but his father denied him that love because he didn't want the women to corrupt him with their belief in Faeries. And then, Malton became his father. Just as loud and bossy, and just as afraid of what he didn't understand. Yes, he realized now, that his father had been afraid. It was the only power that his wife had had, but she seemed to have lost that power when her husband stole her son. His sisters were all married now, and his mother was alone in the West Wing of their huge castle. What she did there, he did not know. He hadn't seen her in almost a year. His father hadn't even let her come to him when he had been so ill. He began to realize who he had become as he followed the Faeries and birds deeper into the woods. He gave the horse his head and he fell deeper into his reflection.

He thought of how he had treated women, servants and everyone. He now remembered that when he was a small boy, he swore he would not become like his father. But he had! He had become exactly like his father. He was approaching a clearing now. In fact, it was a circle—a ring—a Faerie Ring. The stories his mother had whispered to him were now returning to his memory.

At first when he entered the Faerie Ring, he could see nothing. Perhaps it was because he was only on the edge of it.

He decided that he should dismount. It seemed more respectful. He did so, and the horse quickly backed away from the ring. Malton stepped more deeply into the ring. Still he saw nothing. But he felt his sword hang heavy on his thigh. Yes, he must enter in peace if he wished an audience. He removed his sword, which made him feel completely naked, and left it on a stump at the edge of the Faerie Ring.

Gradually, a vision formed before him. He saw that all the birds and small faeries that he had followed were just inside the ring in a large circle. The larger birds often had small faeries of different colors riding on their backs. Hawks were next to sparrows, and small rabbits and rodents were grouped at the feet of foxes. Just before him, he saw a magnificent white stag with a garland of jasper around his neck, and next to him was an empty throne. Beside it was another one. Upon that throne was his Faerie Woman!

"Your Highness," he said as he dropped to one knee. To the right of the Faerie woman was a beautiful doe with a garland of flowers about her neck.

"Arise, my lord," spoke Shature in her lilting voice. "Your place is ready."

She pointed to the throne beside her.

"Where is my son?" growled the King to his wife. He had entered her chambers for the first time in months.

"Lord, please, sit," she said calmly. "You are just in time for tea."

"Bah—I don't drink the stuff. Don't try to distract me. Where is our son?"

"Oh, now he is our son?"

The Queen remained calm and reached for her cup of tea.

"It's your fault." He roared. "You fed all that nonsense into his mind when he was a boy. Now he has gone into the west woods in search of some Faerie woman."

"I know," returned his wife in her usual calm voice. "In fact, I heard that you sent him."

"Nonsense. I told him to stay away from those woods."

"But you know he always does the opposite of what he is told. Now you want to blame me. I'm sorry, I can be of no assistance to you."

The King looked totally out of place in the Queen's chambers as he grumbled and groaned at her. She had had the West Wing to herself since she finally birthed him a son. Then, he had left her alone. She was glad. She had made a life for herself. She had raised her daughters and saw her son as much as possible. That is, until he lost all interest in her. He had become just like his father. She had tried to tell him of his destiny, but his father had stopped her at every turn. The Queen had always been very unhappy with the King, especially when she had been obliged to bear him a son. By the fifth daughter, she was desperate for a boy. Otherwise that man would never leave her alone. Her father had made her marry him, to seal a treaty and to punish her for falling in love with a commoner. Actually, he was not a commoner. He was a Faerie. It was to her Faerie lover that she had gone for help. He gave her many charms and potions, but the next two children were also girls.

"What am I to do?' she cried in his arms, for they had remained lovers all those years. He could materialize in certain places in her living quarters where she had prepared the energy. She could never have gone all the way to the Enchanted Forest without being discovered.

"I can give you a son," said her Faerie lover.

She looked to him in the love that had only grown over the years. "You could? But no, it wouldn't work. You are dark haired and my husband and I are both as light as our daughters. The boy must look like him."

"That can be accomplished."

"But why have you never told me this before?' She said in an angry voice "I have had to suffer that oaf all these years."

Her lover embraced her.

"My dear, the timing was not right and you were not ready. It is difficult for a member of Faerie and an Earth human to mate because their vibrations are so very different. We vibrate at a much higher frequency than humans do. That is why only you can see me. The others about you have a much lower consciousness. But because you are part faerie, you can see me. And since we have been lovers all these earth years, our vibrations have grown very sympathetic. I think that now we could conceive a child together."

"What?" she replied in shock to her lover's statement that she was part faerie.

"Yes, your mother also fell in love with one of our men, as did her mother and so on for many generations back. That is the true reason why you were sent to marry this man. It was your destiny."

"My destiny?"

"Yes, your husband's kingdom is on the edge of our land, and he is a non-believer. He has lowered the vibration of his kingdom with his lecherous and greedy acts. He recognizes and advances only those like himself, and they do the same. You see, one man can make a very big difference, either to the good or to the bad. Your son—our son—shall change that."

And so it was done. And indeed the baby was light of hair and blue of eyes. The King was overcome with joy. Destiny had begun. But it seemed to go awry. The boy was taken from his mother and sisters and was turned into the same oaf as his father.

"Where are you now?" moaned the King. "You have gone off into your fantasy world again. You see, it is your doing. I tried to protect my son from your weak mind, but now you have won."

"I have not won. Our son has gone to seek his destiny."

"Destiny—Bah—he is ill and enchanted by your godless faeries. I will find him if I have to burn down the forest!"

With those final words, he stomped from her quarters, leaving mud stains on her fine linen rugs. The Queen was worried. She must find a way to warn her son."

"Why did you make me wander through these woods so long before you presented yourself?" said Malton, as he lay upon a fallen log with his head upon Shature's lap.

They had just made love – again. They resided not in the Faerie that Shature had known with Tamara and the changers, but a lower vibration of Faerie where the energies were not quite as high as the Kingdom of Faerie, but above the vibration of Earth. This area was often known as the Borderland, and those who knew how could reach both the Earthly kingdom and the Faerie Kingdom. Shature had learned how to raise her vibration again so that she could return to Tamara, the changers and Violet, but she could not raise Malton's vibration. He had to learn how to do that for himself, and she doubted that he ever would.

Malton was no longer angry, and he was no longer enchanted. He was in love and enjoying it. He found he loved loving Shature more than drinking, more than cavorting with his men, definitely more than whoring, and even more than fighting. At least for now. Shature had given herself to him totally. He had "made love" for the first time in his life. Always before he had taken a woman without a single thought for her needs. But with Shature, he wanted to please her as much as she pleased him. And she pleased him very much.

"Our vibrations were too different and you refused to believe that someone like me existed," Shature cooed as she stroked his golden hair. "I did try to show myself, but you didn't see me. I appeared in your dreams, but you didn't remember them. You were too filled with mead and anger to hear my call or see my face. Finally, when you were ill from your injury, your hallucinations released you from your father's indoctrination."

"My father," pondered Malton. "What would he think if he knew I was here with you? I am sure he is sick with anger and worry by now. I mustn't stay here too long. He could cause you and your people harm."

"But, you aren't planning to leave are you?" Shature cried as she stood up and unceremoniously dumped Malton onto the forest floor.

"Of course, my Love. I am to be King someday. I can't spend my life playing in the woods with you. I have responsibilities."

"Playing in the woods!" she cried. "We have created a kingdom here which is between Earth and Faerie that will further heal the connection between the two lands. Remember our work in Faerie and the long life we shared there? We are Complements. You have responsibilities here, too."

Malton stood as well and took both of Shature's hands in his. He looked into her tear filled eyes as he spoke.

"I am sorry, Love, but I do not remember our time in Faerie and I do not understand what a Complement is. Look, you have changed my life and showed me that there is another kingdom that coexists with my own. You have shown me how to respect the nature that we both share and I have fallen deeply in love with you. Isn't that enough?"

Shature wanted to argue, but she knew he was right. He had his destiny and she must not interfere with it. Perhaps, now they could communicate between Earth and Faerie as they had done before. He would eventually shed his earthen shell and return to her in Faerie.

"You are right, my love," she cooed. "When will you have to return?"

"No, no—WE will return! You are to be my Queen. I could have no one else after you. You are my Divine Complement."

"Malton, a moment ago, you did not know what that meant. Now you are using it to bring me to your world. I have responsibilities too."

"But you are a woman. Your responsibility is to give me a son!"

"NEVER!!" She stood up and strode off into the forest where he could not find her.

"She is just playing hard to get," he thought. "She will change her mind. I will make her."

Their fight continued for days and days. However, days in their Faerie Borderland were different than days on Earth and much Earth time had now passed. The King had indeed tried to burn down the forest, but the few men he could summon to enter the Enchanted Forest were so terrified by the visions they saw that they ran away. Then the faeries called rain to put out the fires before much damage could be done. Wherever, the men lit a fire, it would rain in that location only until the fire was put out. Finally, the King gave up. He knew that his son would come to his senses soon and return to rule his kingdom. But, much time passed and his son did not come. The King lost all joy in his life and began to waste away. His robust form became thinner and thinner. Even the Queen was worried about him. Her son must return now. His father would not last much longer, and then who would rule the kingdom?

Finally, she made a brave move. She called her Faerie lover to lead her into the Enchanted Forest. The King was so distraught now that he would not notice her absence. In fact, if he knew, he would probably allow her to go. He was that upset.

"Oh, my Love, I cannot take you there. Humans cannot return."

"But I am half faerie and my son is three quarters Faerie. He must follow his destiny. He can have her as a lover as I have had you."

"My dear, he may be largely Faerie, but he was raised a human and still does not have his Faerie vision. He will want to possess her, as all human men do."

"I will talk to him."

"Pardon my saying so, my love, but he hasn't listened to you in years."

"Yes, but he is a man in love. He may listen to me now."

And so they went into the woods. Shature knew what was happening and was tempted to interfere so that the Queen would never find them, but she heard the voice of Tamara warning her that it is dangerous to interfere with someone else's destiny. Perhaps it was time for Malton to leave. She couldn't make him leave without her. Maybe his mother could. She only knew that nothing could make her leave.

"Mother, how did you get here?" Malton was shocked.

"I have come to take you home, son. Your father is gravely ill and you are needed to fulfill his duties."

"But mother, you are the one who told me of Faerie. Why are you asking me to leave it?"

"It is your duty, dear. Your father was disrespectful of this hidden world. Now that you have learned of it and learned to care for it as I do, you can rule our people in harmony with the Faerie Kingdom."

"Yes, mother, you are right. But I have fallen in love and I have vowed not to return unless she is by my side."

The Queen remembered her lover's words. She must be careful in how she proceeded.

"Let me speak to her, Malton. Perhaps she will listen to the voice of a woman."

The Queen had decided not to tell Malton of his true identity, but she did tell Shature.

"You see, Shature, this plan has been activated by higher sources than any of us here, long, long ago. I know my son, he will not leave without you. Please come back with him. Then, when all is settled, you can return to Faerie. I promise that my friend, Malton's real father, and I will help."

The Queen's impassioned speech changed Shature's mind, where Malton's boasting could not. They set out immediately.

"Malton, you must promise me that you will allow me to return to these woods every full moon and every solstice."

"Yes, my love, and you must promise me that you will then return to me."

Shature stopped. "NO! I cannot promise that. I never bound you to stay in the woods and I will not leave here if you bind me to your rock castle."

The Queen rolled her eyes. Love was such a problem. She could see that these two would awaken their boring, masculine castle.

"Please, children," she interceded. "Must you continuously fight. Malton, I think she is right."

"But a wife must stay with her husband until death."

"Malton, she is not your wife yet. Please, your father needs you. I am sure that you can convince her to marry you later," she said as she winked at Shature.

It was not until they reached the edge of the forest that Malton could see the state of his kingdom. There were once fertile pastures that edged the woods. Now they were overgrown in brambles with no sheep in sight. As they rode closer and closer to the castle, they could see how the entire kingdom had suffered in his absence.

"How long has father been ill?" asked Malton to his mother in deep concern.

"Almost since you left over seven years ago."

"Seven years, but I was only gone a few months." He turned to Shature in anger. "Why didn't you tell me?"

"I did," she replied, "but you wouldn't listen to me."

She was right, of course, but he would not believe that they actually were on a different dimension or that time could be different in each dimension.

"But we just rode out," he said. "How could we have come from such a different place so quickly?"

"Malton," Shature answered. "You only see what you expect and believe in. I have been performing chants and incantations throughout our entire journey, but you did not wish to see. You are still afraid of a reality that is so different form your own."

"Bah—afraid. I am a great warrior. Nothing frightens me."

If it weren't for the Queen, Shature would have returned to her sacred Faerie right then and there. But the Queen gave her such a plaintive look that she stayed. However, she knew that she could not stay in this harsh land. Already Malton was different. He was back to the person he had been before their meeting in the Enchanted Forest. And, already, she could feel that she was different as well. Vague memories of how she had felt in Atlantis returned to her. But now she was with her Divine Complement, and he was human. She did not like the human part of him, and she did not like the human part of herself. She thought she had forgiven Atlantis, but she had not forgiven the vibration of humanity. How could she live in a world that neglected nature because the King was ill? How could she be in a place where women and men were treated differently? She decided then and there, she would not marry him!

Oh, but Love was more powerful than she could imagine. The King's health made a comeback when Malton returned, but it was not permanent. He died within a few months. Malton was saddened by the loss of his father, but he buried his emotions in his work. Now he was King, and his kingdom had been neglected for seven years. In public Malton was almost like his father, except that he believed in and protected Faerie. But in private, he was like Lamire and was as tender and loving as he had ever been in Faerie. He confided everything to Shature and was ever loyal to her. Shature insisted that the mead stay under control and that he sleep in her bed -- not in the Great Hall. But when he was King, he was gruff and loud. He yelled orders and drank with his soldiers. She hated that part of him, or did she love it? The polarities were so strong on this dimension. Good was very good and bad was very bad. Even the light of the Sun was brighter and much more direct and the dark of a moonless night was darker than any darkness in Faerie.

In fact, Shature could not help but compare the differences between life on Earth, which was the third dimension, life on Faerie, which was the fourth dimension, and life on Venus, which was the fifth dimension. When she was in Faerie with Lamire, she was so content that she seldom thought of Venus. But now that she was on Earth again, and even with her Complement, she often thought of Home. When she was with Lamire on Venus, they were one being. Now they were still of the same Soul, but they were completely different in their expressions of it. When she and Lamire were together in the Faerie Kingdom, they had separate forms, but their hearts and minds were one. Now, the only time that she and Lamire, now known as Malton, felt united in that way was when they made love.

Sex was also very different here than on the higher dimensions. In Faerie, sex was for fun and, if their bodies had been harmonized and prepared, it was also for procreation. On Venus, sex was an orgasmic experience of the Cosmic All. This experience was saved for only the most spiritual of rituals of either stepping into the Violet Flame together to bring down a new Soul for embodiment or for raising consciousness to unite with higher portions of one's self. Since most Venusians were androgynous, living in one form with their Complement, sex was a form of meditation rather than a form of physical coupling. Two complete, androgynous souls would share the experience of bringing down another Soul to be loved and raised by their entire community, or they could assist each other in raising their consciousness as well as the group consciousness of the community.

When Shature had viewed Malton from her place in Faerie and from seeing the lives of the other members of his kingdom, it appeared that sex was often for power. On Earth, sex was often a mating drive like the animals in the forest, except that a female animal had the right to refuse. This right was not always granted to human females. This kind of sex was neither fun nor enjoyable. Sexual encounters seemed impulsive and without forethought. New souls were brought down into physical form with no planning or preparation, and the honor of parenthood was often reduced to a grim duty. Shature saw that many parents were mere children themselves and completely unprepared to offer their child a happy or fulfilling life.

Shature would only mate with Malton in the Enchanted Forest. The vibration was much higher there and she had felt much safer than in Malton's rock castle. She could not forget the images of him taking many other women, wherever he pleased. She would not be in that category. She would be with him sexually only if he was kind and patient and raised his consciousness above the role of "dominating King". In the Enchanted Forest, they were in her world. He instantly softened there and she felt in her power. She did not enjoy the "beds" of the humans and felt much more at ease on the forest floor. He sometimes became angry when she demanded that they go into the forest to make love, but she would not sleep with him if he did not respect her wishes. Actually, he greatly enjoyed their trips into the forest, and he also knew that if he ever forced her to have sex with him, she would leave him. Malton knew that Shature loved him deeply, but he did not know if her love was strong enough for her to stay in his land, which was foreign and inhospitable to her.

Shature knew that Malton could sense her inner conflict, and this made her love him even more. She was having difficulty adjusting again to the simplest aspects of life on the third dimension. For example, eating seemed like a new experience to her. In Faerie, eating food was for fun and friendship, and on Venus it was a form of uniting with and partaking of the Cosmic All. On Venus, their forms were light bodies and nourishment was the vibration of light taken in through the process of breathing. On Earth, however, eating was a basic survival need. Those of money, means and power often ate far too much, while the poor around them lived just above the starvation level. Shature made sure that everyone in her service and physical area had enough to eat. She would regularly send out her servants with any extra food so that those who were hungry would not go without food. However, the word spread and there were so many at her door begging for food that she had to instead create work to be done so that they could earn their food.

Shature was also unfamiliar with the concept of "work". On the Earth plane, one had to work hard, or command someone else to work hard, in order to get what he or she needed. In Faerie, desires were filled by ritual and magic, and on Venus there was complete freedom from all desire because all lived in abundance consciousness. In abundance consciousness, one did not desire. They simply manifested what was necessary at that moment, and allowed it to return to the Oneness when it was no longer needed. Shature did not feel comfortable having servants who dressed, washed, and fed her and lived to fulfill her every need. Her magic skills were still very much intact, and she could manifest for herself whatever she desired. However, she found that she had to do this in private, as there was much fear of the unknown. Also, women were not supposed to have power. They were to obey their men completely and could only rule over other women. Luckily, Shature had the Queen for a dear friend.

Shature took many trips into the forest where she could open the vortex into Faerie. She returned there often and gained much from her visits. Malton did not wish her, a woman, to leave the castle unescorted and insisted that she was chaperoned by at least two well-armed guards. However, she went to the woods alone as often as she could. She did not understand nor respect the different rules for men and women. In Faerie, there was still the separation of male and female, but everyone knew that they had a Complement and that they would eventually meet them. Men and women were both completely independent, and all roles and responsibilities were determined by desires rather than by gender. On Venus, most of the people in her community had chosen to be androgynous and therefore, there was no male or female. Each being was seen as a body of light in complete equality and love. Some appeared more feminine or masculine, but in actuality they were both. There were elders, of course, but everyone knew that they too would achieve that status as they progressed in their spiritual endeavors.

Shature missed the unity consciousness of Venus where each Soul viewed itself as a component of the One. There were no thoughts of separation or limitation there, nor was there comparison or competition. Even in Faerie, where the polarities were stronger than on Venus, there was a constant sense of cooperation and sharing, at least in her community. In Malton's kingdom, and from what she could determine the third dimensional world around her, every person felt separate, even from their loved ones. There was love that brought cohesiveness to family and community, but even that was often filled with fear and suspicion.

But the difference that caused her the most embarrassment was the differences in time and space. On Venus, there was no time and space. There was only the moment and the place that one was in at that moment. Although very different from Earth, there was still the concept of time and space on Faerie. One would travel from one "place" to another and the journey took "time". On Venus, one was in a place at one moment and then, if they desired to change experiences, they would change their thoughts and they were instantly wherever their thoughts took them. There was no experience of traveling from one location to another unless that was the particular experience that was desired. "Time" in Faerie was relative to the activity. When the activity was enjoyable there seemed to be no passage of time. But when the activity was not enjoyable, time seemed to pass more slowly. Therefore, few beings in Faerie performed any activity that they did not enjoy. Shature, still being very much her Faerie self, did not abide by the strict time schedule of castle life. She was usually late, or did not appear at all. Then a servant was sent to find her. Shature had planned to be where they awaited her, but she could not keep track of the movement of time in such a regimented fashion.

The reality was that Shature did not want to keep track of her obligations as Malton's woman. She was her own woman and she had no desire to be, or to act like, "his Queen". Malton's mother started to take over the Queen's obligations. This was still acceptable because Shature had not yet married Malton, but it had been almost a year since she had come to live with Malton, and she would have to marry him soon or return to Faerie.

Shature did not like her life on Earth, but she loved Malton. Their relationship grew closer and closer as he understood and accepted her more with each passing day. They had wonderfully intimate communications in the Enchanted Forest and in their castle garden, which grew to great proportions under Shature's care. He stopped asking her to make love with him while they were in bed, which had the affect of allowing her to begin to desire it. Perhaps she was being unfair and controlling. But she also knew that making love only in the Forest was also a form of birth control. While they were members of Faerie, procreation was something that needed to be prepared for on a vibrational level. It was not just the unplanned for consequence of sex that it was on Earth. She knew that if she were with child that her decision would be even more difficult.

One night, after they'd had a particularly intimate discussion filled with laughter and joy, she confided her desire to make love with him while in bed. She also shared her fears of an unwanted child.

"I would want the child," he said as he looked deep into her eyes.

She felt his love and sincerity deep in her heart.

"My beloved," he continued, "I know how difficult it is for you in my world. I only wish that I could remember the life that you say we shared on Faerie. I know that I am a harsh brute sometimes, but your love heals me more with each day. However, I am committed to the life that I have taken here. It may not be as wondrous as the life we shared in Faerie, but it is a good life. Because of you, I realize that I have a real opportunity to help others. Was that not the reason we chose to come here from Venus? You, my love, are still afraid of that choice. When you volunteered to come to Earth, did you not mean the physical plane? I know that you suffered greatly in Atlantis and that you say you miss the higher vibrations which are more akin to your spirit, but didn't you also make a commitment to assist in the changes of this planet?

"You say that you have forgiven your past, but I cannot agree with that. If you have truly forgiven your past you would be able to live in the present. This life - this castle - is your present, yours and mine together! I want nothing more than to share it with you. I know that you would like me to return to Faerie with you, but my love, I cannot do that. It is here that my work is and I believe that it is your work as well. Think of the wonderful child that we could conceive. Think of the wonderful children! Allow me darling, to show you the deep joys of physical love just as you have shown me the joys of love in Faerie."

He then held her close to him as he released her hair from its braid. Shature's long hair fell long and flowing across her back. He pulled it together and laid its shimmering tresses between her breasts.

"I love your hair," he whispered as he kissed it from her shoulders, between her breasts and down to her waist where it curled across her navel.

His kisses then followed her hair back to her bosom where he gently untied her nightgown, lace, by lace, by lace. Gently, he pulled the gown back across her shoulders, leaving her naked to her waist. He nuzzled his face in her hair and down to her waist as he gently pulled the gown across her naked stomach and thighs. He kissed her gently on each area of skin as it was exposed.

He sat up and pulled off his shirt and then his pants. He had done these things many times on the forest floor, but somehow it felt different this time. In this plane of polarities where the negative was very evident and the pain very harsh, the pleasure was also more intense. Shature quivered under his kisses and his gentle touch. The possibility that they could conceive a child created an element of fear and excitement not present when they made love in the Enchanted Forest. He spoke to her constantly in a quiet loving voice, reassuring her that he would be a responsible father and that she would be a wonderful mother. And then, gradually, as the passion mounted, she was no longer a potential mother, but rather the object of his deepest desires. His kisses became urgent and filled with lust. She loved it. She loved being taken by him and she loved being seduced. She understood for the first time the concept of being a woman in the third dimension. She understood why the women longed to be protected and cared for. She wanted to surrender to him. She wanted to fall into him and experience the humanness in him that she had feared before. His kisses became hot and hers were just as filled with lust. She allowed her Faerie vibration to mingle with her clay body that had subtlety grown denser during her time in Malton's world.

Shature felt such a great fire growing in her body that she did not know if she could contain it. She knew Malton also had that fire and that he struggled to master it and remain gentle with her. Suddenly, she did not need him to be gentle. She needed him to release his essence within her. She wanted to know his physical self inside of her in a way that was only possible on the third dimension. He was right. She had been afraid. She was afraid of her passion and judged it as physical weakness. Now she wanted to explore her body and his as well. Malton was becoming so passionate that he could barely control himself. And, to her surprise, she did not want him to.

"Do it," she cried. "Come into me with all your fire and all your passion. I love you. I accept you -- all of you. You are of the animal, as am I. We are two separate portions of the same essence. I want to feel all of you inside me."

He did not need her to ask him twice. He instantly entered her quivering body and the thrill of it almost forced an early release. But he contained himself. He wanted her to enjoy it as much as he. And she was enjoying it, more than she could ever imagine. She knew now that she *could* allow him to take her on the floor of the Great Hall or across the table of the Council Room. And she knew she would enjoy it. Shature was now a part of his body and a part of his life.

Slowly, with controlled passion, Malton moved within her until she began to pant and moan. Their bodies became one again. His arms were a part of her body and her arms a part of his. Again there was no separation between them. They were entangled in a mounting flame that built to such a crescendo that they both cried out in joy when they reached orgasm together. Even then they stayed intertwined. Malton did not relax his embrace of her nor did he leave her side. He held her to him with a tender yet firm protectiveness. He pushed her damp hair away from her body that was drenched with sweat as was his. As they fell off to sleep together, he whispered into her ear.

"Welcome to *my* world, beloved."

He allowed her to go into the Enchanted Forest as he had promised, but every time it grew more and more difficult for her to find and open the vortex into Faerie. Then one day she knew that she had to decide once and for all which world she would live in. It was Tamara who told her. It had taken a long time for her to find the vortex and it took many rituals before she could open it.

"This will be your last trip here, Shature. If you return, you shall not be able to open the vortex again."

"But why?" cried Shature.

"You are with child. It is too difficult for the unborn to make the transition. If you give birth to the child here, which you may, you will have to leave Malton. The time frame for bearing the child here will take many years in Malton's life and he will have lost his wife and his child. However, if you bear your child on Earth, your vibration will become so dense that you will no longer be able to open the vortex. Which do you choose?"

"I can't make that decision so quickly."

"Time is already passing on Earth. The time-space differentials are too difficult for an unborn child."

Shature was struck with many conflicting emotions. She had thought that she might be with child, but she had refused to think of the consequences of that. In her denial, she was becoming more like Malton. Could she leave him now and deny him his child? No! Of course she could not! She had started something and now she must finish it.

"You knew this all along, didn't you, Tamara?"

"I knew the possibility of it. You have a free will as a human. You could have made it different."

"But how? How could I have made it different?"

Tamara smiled. "I will see you soon, Shature."

"But it won't be soon for me."

"Remember, Shature, you have free will. You can create your own life!"

Shature could not respond or say good bye to her friends or even to Violet. The vortex formed around her and Tamara faded from her vision.

"Malton will have a child," were her last thoughts.

She awoke in her bed with Malton's concerned face before her.

"Oh, my darling, I was so concerned. When you did not return on time I raced into the woods and I found you on the forest floor where you lay unconscious. That was yesterday. I have been so worried."

As he spoke he held her so close that he almost crushed her.

"Be careful, Malton," she said. "You will harm our child!"

Malton could not take the joy of finding her alive and having a child at the same time. He hid his face in her lap and sobbed like a baby. Shature stroked his long golden hair and looked around the room.

"This is to be my home now," she thought. "I am human."

Then her eyes caught a small vase on the nightstand beside her bed. In it was a violet flower.

"Where did you find that flower?" she excitedly asked Malton.

He collected his emotions and gave her a quick kiss before he sat up and answered.

"Why, it was beside you on the forest floor. I took it as a good omen and brought it home."

Many years later…

Shature gradually returned to consciousness to see the worried faces of her large family in varying stages of grief. Why were they so upset, and why were they all here in her bedroom? She tried to speak to them but found that she could not utter a word. She tried to move her hand, but could not. What was wrong with her? Just a moment ago, she and her beloved Lamire were flying through the lovely meadows of Faerie. How Shature had missed Faerie, and how she had missed Lamire. No wait, he had another name. His name was—yes—it was Malton. But Malton had died. Slowly she realized that now she was dying too. At least she was dying to the portion of herself that was lying in the bed.

Shature wished that she could speak. She wanted to assure her loved ones that she was still very much alive and was simply changing her consciousness to another portion of her total self. She had tried to remember her higher selves through her long life as Queen, wife, and mother, but her many responsibilities had made her forget much of her higher wisdom. What she remembered, she shared with all who would listen. Her children listened to her stories with rapture when they were young, but usually "grew out of them" as they matured.

Shature had lived many years as Malton's wife. She had twelve children, but only eight of them had survived into adulthood, and four of those had preceded her in death. Two of her sons had died in battle, one son had died of an illness, and a daughter had died in childbirth. There had been good times and bad times, but always her family and friends surrounded her. Malton had died seven lonely years ago, and now it was his spirit form who came to her deathbed just as her spirit had often gone to his. Shature was glad that death was coming to her quickly. Malton had been ill for over three years before he finally released his physical form.

Shature was brought back from her remembrances by the cry of one of her many grandchildren. She smiled in her Soul, but did not know whether her body responded. Shature could feel herself floating above it now. She wished that she could say a parting word to each of her loved ones, but after her terrible headache, she had been unable to speak or move her body.

At this death, Shature could not help but remember her other death long ago in the ancient land of Atlantis. How different this life had been. This time she had learned to love the physical world and learned that the polarities of Earth created a deep penetration of life so that one could identify and release old and hidden resistances. In Faerie, she had resisted her fear and, it had silently grown in places so deep inside of her that she could not find them until she took on a physical form again. Had she faced and healed all of that fear in this life? She would have to wait until she met with her Spirit Guides before that question could be answered.

Suddenly, Shature heard a loud noise that sounded like something had crashed to the floor. She looked down at the small form she was leaving and realized that the noise was the collapse of the life force that had once lived within that body. The next sound she heard was the tinkling of a million bells while she felt a blaze of golden light embrace and caress her new formless form.

Shature looked one last time at the many people she had loved and who had loved her. A small child of about three, one of her favorite grandchildren, pointed up to her and laughed. The child's mother, Shature's daughter, was crying too hard to notice the child or to see where she pointed. All the others in the room focused their attention on the empty shell that had once been the home of Shature's consciousness.

All except one. The Spirit of Lamire had come to retrieve his loved one. Lamire smiled brightly in his ethereal form and took Shature's hand. Slowly, the scene beneath them blurred as they returned Home — together!

To be continued...

Visions from Venus

BOOK TWO

The Violet Temple

(Shature studies in the fifth dimensional Violet Temple to re-experience and heal the third and fourth dimensional lives that she lived with her Divine Complement.)

Return to the Fifth Dimension

VENUS

Facing the Darkness

GUILT

Visions from Venus

BOOK THREE

Initiations

(Shature relives her third dimensional lives in which she was able to reunite with her Divine Complement and return to the fifth dimension.)

Remembering Multidimensional Consciousness

I AM

The Call of Mother Earth

THE INNER GODDESS

Epilogue

Recognition of Completion

ABOUT THE AUTHOR

Suzan Caroll has a Ph.D. in clinical psychology, has been a psychotherapist for over 16 years, and has been a student of metaphysics for decades. She lives in Los Angeles by the ocean with her husband and four birds. She has two grown children and one grandson.

To learn more about Suzan and her writings, please visit her Website at:

www.multidimensions.com

Printed in the United States
44295LVS00004B/98

9 780759 616783